JOURNEY TO JEOPARDY

ROCKY MOUNTAIN SAINT BOOK 1

B.N. RUNDELL

WOLFPACK
PUBLISHING
--- est. 2013 ---

Journey To Jeopardy
(Rocky Mountain Saint Book 1)

B.N. Rundell

Wolfpack Publishing

6032 Wheat Penny Avenue

Las Vegas, NV 89122

Cover Design by L.J. Martin

Patience. Described in the Bible as long-suffering. As I think of my life's partner, the expression the patience of a Saint would certainly apply. While I sit at the keyboard, rattling away in my time machine and experiencing the exploits of my protagonist, she waits for me to ask, "Can you listen?" At the conclusion of every chapter, she patiently listens as I read my most recent efforts at writing and she will invariably say, "I like it!" as I breathe a sigh of relief. Oh sure, there are times she corrects or encourages, but it's those patient periods of silence that tell the most. And for well over half a century, she has been more than patient with me and my doings. What an amazing woman. No wonder I love her and, wonder of wonders, she loves me. What a deal!

CHAPTER ONE
REFLECTION

THE WARY WHITETAIL BUCK TIPTOED BETWEEN THE LOW hanging branches of the big oak that spread its shade to the grassy bank of the nearby stream. One step, freeze, scan, lift a hoof and slowly move it forward, cautious of any danger or threat to his quest for water. Another step, freeze and scan. His neck outstretched with his head lowered below shoulder height, his rack bore three tines on each side, some scarred by conflict or challenge from another buck. Believing he was safe, he slowly raised his head, continually scanning the thick forest around him and, feeling confident, he casually strolled to the water and lowered his head for a long drink. Unseen by the royalty of the forest, a tousle-headed boy, young man really, watched from his hideaway beyond an alder bush. The boy, Tatum Saint, watched the tawny-coated deer, enjoying the proximity, and observed. He held a longbow and sported a buckskin quiver full of steel-tipped arrows crafted in the workshop under the tutelage of his father, an English history buff and sometime school teacher. He was proud of the workmanship of his father and what he had learned from him as they worked to duplicate the longbows of the archers of the British Isles. *"They were the real warriors of their time; why, it was the archers that turned the tide against the French in the Hundred Years War. If it hadn't been for them, Britain would have fallen and we'd all be speakin' French now!"*

Tatum chuckled to himself as he thought of his father. Johnathan St. Michaels—they dropped the Michaels part when the family immigrated to America from the Isle of Man —had been a respected headmaster at a school in Cape Girardeau before his mother died. He could never forgive his wife for tending to the smallpox stricken children in the Osage Indian village and succumbing to the disease herself. Demon Rum, as his mother used to call it, had been the downfall of his father, causing him to lose his position at the most respected and historical school in the Cape. And when he heard of the settlement that would become Springfield and that they were wanting to start a school, Johnathan and Tatum packed up their few belongings and traveled west to the beginnings of a small community of farmers. They settled into a newly built one room log cabin, built a small workshop and lean-to for their horses, and things went well for a while.

The first year, Johnathan conducted classes for the few children, five to be exact, in his home. The other settlers made promises about building a proper school but what with putting in crops, clearing land, building cabins, and all the other jobs of a new settlement, the schoolhouse remained nothing more than a promise. Johnathan made it a point: "Well, if I can't teach the other children, I will teach you everything I know and we'll learn much more together." Tatum didn't mind; he enjoyed learning, especially when that learning involved hands-on work with a longbow and arrows, or building furniture, or helping with a cabin, or practical things like hunting and fishing. He also enjoyed reading. It was a way of escape to distant lands and other times, and even the writings of the ancient philosophers and intellectuals were interesting in their own way. But it was what he considered practical that appealed to him most of all and now, as he observed the buck taking its fill, he thought this was the practical kind of learning, observing life in the forest.

Tatum made friends easily and his first friend at their new home was from the nearby farm of a family of Osage Indians. Red Calf was the oldest son of Jeremiah Tallchief and was just a year older than Tatum but considerably taller. The Osage were known for their unusually tall stature, with many reaching well over six feet and a few were known to be as tall as seven feet; Red Calf, at fifteen, was already close to six feet, making him half a head taller than Tatum. Before coming to their new home, Tatum thought he was taller than most boys his age but Red Calf often kidded him for being so short. The boys had bonded right off and spent most of their free time together in the woods. But Tatum regularly visited the home of his friend and being more inquisitive than most, learned many of the ways and skills of the Osage. The buckskin britches and shirt and moccasins he now wore were made with the guidance of Red Calf and his father.

Johnathan had also visited the Tallchief family but their conversation had been about history and their Christian faith which was the reason Red Calf's father had taken the name Jeremiah. Because they owned the land of their farm, the Tallchief family was not subject to the Indian Removal act of 1830 and was able to stay in their home. He said the Osage leaders had requested missionaries and a Presbyterian missionary had taught him the English language and about Jesus and encouraged him to become a Christian. Tallchief said he had taught his family about Jesus and they were all proud to be Christians. Johnathan told Tatum he enjoyed visiting with the Tallchief family more than with most of the white families in the area and encouraged Tatum to learn from the Osage. "What you learn from them will not only help you in the woods but in your life as well."

Tatum's attention was brought back to the buck and it raised its head suddenly and instantly sprang back into the thick woods, quietly disappearing into the shadowy forest. Tatum moved only his eyes as he searched for the cause of the buck's alarm, taking shallow breaths, unmoving. A slight rustle of leaves brought his focus to the narrow trail beside the big oak and he saw the waddling form of a badger moving toward the water. Tatum waited until the badger reached the water's edge, stepped into his bow as his father taught him, and released the arrow that whispered its way to penetrate the thick fur and hide of the badger. With a muted squeal, the impaled rodent dropped flat on its belly and ceased all movement. Tatum waited a moment, knowing the ferocity of the heavy-clawed animal; seeing no sign of life, he slowly walked to his kill. He hadn't taken the deer because they had no need of meat but the fur of the badger would bring cash money at the traders and they could always use cash money.

He poked the carcass with the tip of his bow, then with his foot and, satisfied the animal was dead, he grabbed the hind foot and lifted the heavy rodent away from the bank of the creek. Using his knife, he cut his arrow from the carcass, wiped it off in the grass and, with some struggle, put the carcass in his game bag and started for his home. He hoped his father would be there but all too often lately, his father could be found at the traders with his old friend Demon Rum or some other cheap substitute.

Red Calf stepped into the path before him and Tatum stopped abruptly as he looked at the stern face of his friend. "My father sent me to find you," said Red Calf and turned, expecting Tatum to follow. "Wait! I'm headed home to have supper with my father!" exclaimed Tatum, surprised by his friend's bluntness.

Red Calf turned back to face Tatum and said, "Your father is at the traders and won't be at your house. My father said to bring you to our home for our meal."

Tatum lifted his head slightly in understanding, shrugged his shoulders and motioning to Red Calf said, "Okay, lead out then."

JOHNATHAN SAINT WALKED THE MILE AND A HALF TO THE trader's intending to resupply their coffee and cornmeal and to see if his order from St. Louis had come in yet. But his arrival was before the expected freight wagon so at the invitation of the trader and a couple of men at the lone table, he decided to wait for the freighter and enjoy a little company and maybe a drink or two. It was early afternoon and the muleskinner was expected well before nightfall.

"Hey there, John ol' boy. How 'bout joinin' us in a friendly hand of cards?" drawled a familiar face from the dark corner of the trader's shack. The voice came from Shad Whitcomb, one of the early settlers that had a well-established farm. He was seated at the lone table with another man unknown to Johnathan, but appeared friendly. Johnathan walked to the table, squinted at the two men, and answered, "Well, I'm not a gamblin' man but I reckon a hand or two will pass the time." He seated himself and watched as Shad dealt the cards and noticed the stranger motion to the trader to bring a bottle and some glasses. The stranger introduced himself as a drummer that was passing through and gave his name as Herkimer Jacobson. "Herk, for short, that's what most folks call me anyway," he explained as he held his hand over the table to shake with Johnathan. Shad interjected, "This here's our schoolteacher, Johnathan Saint."

Cash money was scarce in the times and the game was played with a five-cent limit so no one would get too far in the hole. And it was a friendly game to be enjoyed by all. Even old Blue, the trader—though no one knew why he was called Blue and he never gave his real name—would join in for a hand or two as his time and duties allowed. Between hands, Blue asked Johnathan, "So, whatchu plannin' on doin' with that Hawken you ordered? Gonna go findju a buffler?"

"No, but here a while back, I was huntin' with my boy Tatum and shot a deer with that .36 caliber New Bedford flinter. Hit him good, too, but he didn't go down. Had to track that rascal for almost three miles and still had to shoot him again. And that ain't the first time that happened so I decided to get me a big enough rifle that if I hit 'em in the foot it'd kill 'em!"

"Well, that .54 caliber Hawken'll sure do that, an' then some. And you're all paid up so's soon as the freighter gets in, you can take it and skedaddle on home. Lessin' you be wantin' sumpin' else?"

Johnathan gave it a bit of thought and said, "Yessir, believe I will. That's part of what I came in for so I'll be needing some Arbuckles, a couple bars of Galena lead, a bag of corn-meal, and one each of flour and sugar. Oh, and a couple cans of powder. I imagine I'll be using some to get used to that new rifle and pistol, too."

Blue used a stub of pencil, a slip of paper and figured up the bill and passed it to Johnathan who reached into his front pocket and brought out the correct amount in coin and pushed them across the counter to the trader. "That's got 'er covered. I'll get yore stuff together so it'll be ready when the freighter gets here."

"Hey John, you gonna git in on this hyar hand?" called Shad from the table.

With a nod of his head to the card players, Johnathan turned to the table and seated himself in time to cut the cards. As he did, he noticed the bottom card was a king of spades but he thought nothing of it. The drummer dealt the cards announcing, "Five card stud, same limit."

As the play continued, cards were discarded and new ones dealt to complete their hands. The drummer said, "I'll raise fifty cents," and looked at the others.

Shad reminded him, "The limit is five cents. Ain't nobody here gonna play with anything bigger."

"Oh, I forgot. Okay. Then raise it five cents," agreed the drummer.

Both Shad and Johnathan called and the drummer showed his hand. "I've got a full house, kings over treys!"

Johnathan sat up, rubbed his rum-bleared eyes, and looked at the drummer's hand now lying on the table as he pulled in the coins. Johnathan looked up at the drummer, over at Shad, and back at the drummer and said, "Wait a minute. That black king was on the bottom of the deck and the only way it could be in your hand is if you dealt from the bottom. Why would you cheat for a piddlin' pot like that?"

"You better not be callin' me a cheat! I beat you fair an' square!" protested the drummer.

Shad reached for the remaining stack of cards and turned it over to show a five of hearts on the bottom. He looked at Johnathan and asked, "Are you sure, Johnathan?"

Johnathan nodded his head and looked back at the drummer just in time to see him reach under his jacket and bring out a pistol, cocking it as it came. Johnathan pushed back from the table to stand but, slowed by the rum, he staggered and the drummer pulled the trigger. The hammer fell on the cap and the big barreled .50 caliber percussion pistol belched a cloud of grey blue smoke with a roar that rattled the cans on the shelf. The big slug tore through the Lindsey Woolsey shirt of Johnathan, knocking him backwards, stumbling over the downed chair and to the plank floor. Shad and Blue were frozen witnesses but Herkimer Jacobson grabbed the coins on the table and scrambled for the door. He jerked it open and grabbed the reins of his horse and swung into the saddle with a shout to his mount. He slapped leather and dug heels into his mount's ribs. In a quickly rising cloud of dust, he headed for the timber.

Shad and Blue bent over Johnathan and saw him suck in a bloody breath; he looked at Blue and said, "Be sure my boy gets . . ." and his eyes glazed over as he exhaled his last breath.

Shad looked at Blue and said, "Where'd that drummer come from anyway?"

"I dunno, same as any other drummer I guess, probly St. Louis."

"Do ya know what outfit or compny he was with?" asked Shad, standing over the body.

"No, it's the first time I seen him an' he ain't showed me none o' his wares."

Shad shook his head. "And if I know these folks, ain't none of 'ems gonna take time to go chasin' after him. Guess it's just as well. By the time we got anybody together, he'd have a head start an' we'd never catch him. Beats me why anybody'd do such a thing; there weren't more'n thirty cents in that pot!" He looked down at the body of Johnathan, turned to Blue and said, "Alright, help me get him outta here. I'll have to take him home and tell the boy."

The lengthening shadows of the tall hardwood trees at the edge of the clearing told of the lateness of the hour as Shad led his burdened horse toward the small cabin. From a trail into the trees came Tatum, whistling a random tune as he carried the heavy game bag with the badger. He looked up and saw the big farmer leading his horse into the clearing and called out, "Hello, Mr. Whitcomb. What brings you out this late in the day?"

Shad Whitcomb replied, "Hello Tatum," and approached the boy, trying to shield his view of his father's body and continued, "Tatum, son, I've got some bad news for you. Your father was at the traders . . ." and was interrupted when Tatum dropped the bag and ran past him to see the body of his father over the saddle. He lifted his father's head and choked back a sob but fell to his knees and looked through tear-filled eyes to Whitcomb and asked, "How?"

"We was playin' cards, just killin' time waitin' for the freighter. And there was this drummer that cheated and your pa called him on it. And before any of us could do anything, he up and shot your pa and ran off. Sorry, Tatum." He stood by the head of his horse looking at the boy and feeling helpless.

"I always thought somethin' like this'd happen," mumbled Tatum as he looked up at the figure of his father, head hanging by the saddle stirrup.

"You gonna wanna have a service or sumpin'?" asked Shad for lack of anything else to say.

Tatum looked at the man with a blank expression, then nodded his head and said, "Nah, I'll just bury him here by the cabin. That's what he'd want."

"I'll help you, boy. Here, let's get him down and lay him out on the porch yonder," said Shad. The two struggled to carry the dead weight to the porch and laid him gently down. Tatum looked at Shad and said, "You can go on. I'll do it myself."

"You need help, Tatum. That's a big job for a youngster."

"I ain't no youngster an' if you an' the others'd done what

you promised, this wouldn't of happened. He'd stayed home and away from the bottle, tendin' to the school. So, no, I don't need your help," stated Tatum emphatically. He turned away from Whitcomb and started toward the shed to fetch a spade to begin his work. He heard the squeak of saddle leather as Whitcomb mounted and with the rattle of hooves on the hard-packed roadway, he knew he was left alone with the body of his father.

CHAPTER THREE
DECISIONS

HE WORKED WELL INTO THE NIGHT; FORTUNATELY THE SOIL was easy digging and the lamp light sufficient to see through tear-filled eyes. He struggled but was glad for the work to keep his grief at bay. Yet the digging of the grave was just a part of the task he had undertaken by his lonesome. Exhausted, he sat on the porch and leaned back against the side of the cabin, his father's body uncovered by his feet. He looked at the still form and tears carved a pathway down his dirt-encrusted cheeks to fall on his chest. But the boy remained unmoving. He leaned his head back and closed his eyes as fatigue and sleep captured him without resistance.

Lances of bright sunlight stretched over the treetops and brought warmth to the sleeping form of Tatum and he opened his eyes to what he hoped had been a dream. But his father's body was there, and Tatum pulled his legs under him to stand and stretch stiff limbs to ready himself to finish the task. He went into the house and snatched a patchwork quilt from his father's bed and returned to roll the body into its warmth. Although the grave was but ten paces to the side of the cabin, it took Tatum most of half an hour to drag the blanketed form to the edge of the hole. He knew there was no way he could lower the body into the grave; it took all he had to climb out of it last night. So he knelt beside the blanketed mound and said, "Sorry, Pa, but there's just me. So I'm gonna have to roll you in." And he pushed with one hand on the torso and one on the hips, and the body dropped into the grave with a thud and what sounded like a moan. Tatum leaned over the grave with wide eyes, scared he had somehow hurt his father. But realizing it was just the sound of the drop, he stood and grabbed the spade to begin filling in the grave.

He worked, sobbed, shoveled and let the tears blend with the dirt on his face. He sat down on the dirt pile to rest, dropped his head in his hands and began to ponder his future. He had often dreamed of going west with his father and trapping and hunting, exploring the mountains known as the Rockies. But now he was alone and the trip west had been nothing more than the hope of a boy so what was he to do? *I guess I could try farming like the other folks here are doin' but, nah, I ain't no farmer.* He looked up at the sound of someone approaching and saw his friend Red Calf. Tatum wiped at the tears and his hands came away with dirt and mud. He looked up at his friend and watched as Red Calf silently picked up the spade and began throwing dirt into the grave. Tatum relieved his friend and finished making the mound over the grave, patting it firm with the flat of the spade. He walked to the head of the grave and stuck the blade of the shovel into the ground, the handle making a temporary marker. He went to the cabin, returned with his pa's Bible, stood graveside and flipped through the pages. He stopped at Psalm 91:15 and read, *"He shall call upon me and I will answer him; I will be with him in trouble; I will deliver him and honour him. With long life will I satisfy him and shew him my salvation."*

"Well, Pa, you said to let God's word be my guide and this whole chapter says He'll take care of me. So, Pa, I'm goin' west. You know, like we talked. Don't know for sure just what I'll do but I'll be doin' it for the both of us." After a long pause with his head bowed, he said, "G'bye, Pa. Tell Ma I'm alright."

He lifted his eyes to his friend and said, "Red Calf, tell your folks I'll stop by 'fore I leave but, now, I've got to get my things together cuz I'm goin' to the mountains!"

"Are you sure you want to do that? You're not even full growed yet and you ain't never been there, have you?" asked the surprised Red Calf.

"Yup, I'm sure, an' even though I ain't full growed, I can do my growin' up out yonder. 'Sides, 'cept for you and your folks, I'm plumb tired of people and I'd like to get as far away from 'em as I can get," declared the young man.

"Do you need some help? I mean, with gettin' things ready for your journey?"

"I don't rightly know, Red Calf. It's gonna take me a spell to figure out what I need to take and what to leave behind. I know this: whatever is left, you and your folks are welcome to, that is, if you want anything I leave. There's no way I can take everything cuz I only got two horses, mine and Pa's, an' I'll be ridin' one and packin' th' other'n."

He started for the cabin, turned and said, "But first, I gotta go jump in the crick and get some o' this mud off'n me. You wanna go fer a swim?"

Red Calf grinned at his friend and followed him into the cabin. As Tatum rummaged through his stuff in search of something to use as a towel, he said, "I sure wish I had me another set of buckskins. This set is all I'm plannin' on takin', well, after I get 'em washed up at the crick, that is. Say, maybe your ma could give me some pointers on how to sew 'em up an' I can make me some after I get there! I've got some tanned hides out in the shed yonder; maybe I can take them with me and use them."

Red Calf stayed the morning with Tatum and the boys talked about the west and what Tatum might be facing. They discussed what he would definitely need to take as far as supplies and other gear but the piles of taking and leaving grew larger than either expected. Tatum looked at the taking pile and shook his head and said, "Guess I'll have to put more in the leavin' pile cuz I sure can't take all that and my food supplies as well. This is gonna be harder than I thought!"

Red Calf bid his friend good-bye and started on the trail through the thick timber and was soon out of sight. Tatum decided to go to the trader's and get the other supplies he had listed during their planning session. *That way, I'll have a better idea of what I can take and not.* He went to the corral and saddled up his blaze-faced sorrel gelding and started for the trader's. He hadn't left the clearing when he was met by two men, also on horseback, coming toward him. He recognized Shad Whitcomb and, after craning around to see the second man, recognized him as Barnabas Applegate, the village smithy. "Howdy Mr. Whitcomb, Mr. Applegate."

Barnabas spoke first and said, "Tatum, I'm awful sorry about your pa. He was a good man," and Tatum couldn't help but think about what his father had often said about folks always talking respectful of the dead. He had often said, "I find it interesting that even the sorriest rascal is a good man when he's dead."

"Thank you, Mr. Applegate."

"There's something we need to talk to you about, Tatum," said Whitcomb.

"Oh, and what's that?" asked the boy. He could tell the men were uncomfortable about something but he waited for their explanation.

"Well, you see Tatum, we—that is, the village council—

were discussing things and as you know the cabin you and your pa have been livin' in was provided by the village for the schoolteacher. And what with your pa gone now, well, the council wants to see about gettin' another teacher," he looked up at Tatum, trying to judge the boy's reaction before continuing but Tatum interrupted.

"So, what you're doin' here is tellin' me to leave. That right?" asked Tatum, squinting his eyes at the two men.

"Well, not right away understand, but we will be needin' the cabin for the new teacher," explained Applegate.

"Are you gonna make him promises you don't intend to keep like you did my pa?" snapped Tatum. "Never mind, but don't you worry, I'm leavin' here just as soon as I can get packed!" and started to rein his mount past the two men.

Whitcomb said, "Tatum, I'm real sorry about this, I tried to talk them out of it but . . ."

"I know, people that don't keep their promises have a hard time keepin' their word about anything."

As he started past Whitcomb the man said, "Uh, don't forget to get the supplies your pa paid for at the trader's. And don't let old Blue try to cheat you out of that Hawken and that pistol your pa paid for either."

Tatum reined up and looked at the man. "My pa got a Hawken?"

"Yeah, already paid for and waitin' at the trader's. Some other supplies, powder, lead, and other stuff. All paid for. Your pa paid for it while we were waitin' on the freighter to arrive."

"Thanks, Mr. Whitcomb, thanks," muttered Tatum and gigged his horse past the two men on his way to the trader.

CHAPTER FOUR
DICKERING

TATUM STEPPED OFF HIS RED GELDING, LOOSELY TETHERED HIM to the rail, and walked into the trader's cabin. He stopped just inside the door, seeing things with different eyes. No longer the boy with wandering eyes and wondering thoughts, amazed by the myriad of things on the shelves and stacked in piles along the wall, he now looked at the trader leaning on the counter sorting some little tidbits of goods. Blue looked up at the boy and said, "What can I do ye fer, young feller?"

"Well, I'm needin' some supplies for a considerable journey I'm takin'."

"Sounds like yore headed fer a fine adventure. Where 'bouts are you headed?"

"Out west. Goin' to the mountains," declared the young man standing before the counter. "So, first, I think I'll be needin' a new rifle. How 'bout that Hawken there?" he asked as he pointed to the rifle standing upright on the shelf behind the trader.

"Well, that's a mighty fine rifle, maybe a bit big for you, don'tcha think?" asked the trader as he turned to retrieve the rifle and hand it to Tatum.

"No, I think this'll do just fine. Yessir, an' how 'bout that pistol layin' there, is that a Paterson Colt?"

Blue looked at the young man somewhat suspiciously but turned and picked up the pistol to hand to the young man who laid the rifle on the counter. He hefted the pistol, held it at arm's length, sighted down the barrel and said, "Yessir, this'll do fine. Now, I'm gonna need a few other things like powder, caps, lead, flour, sugar, cornmeal, Arbuckles, oh, and don't forget those two bullet molds that go with these," pointing at the rifle and pistol on the counter before him.

Blue looked at the young man and said, "That's quite a bit. Are you shore you got the money to pay for it?"

"Don't you worry about it at all, just gather it up please," said Tatum, smiling.

When Blue had assembled the goods on the counter, he used his stub of a pencil and slip of paper to do his figuring on and, satisfied, pushed the paper to the young man for payment. When Tatum had gone through his father's pockets, he found a similar paper but didn't know what it was at the time but kept it. He now reached into his pocket as if digging for coin but brought out the paper and laid it on the counter beside the one of Blue's. The trader looked at the paper, up at the boy, and started stammering, "Uh, uh, but I didn't know you was Johnathan's boy. Why didn't you tell me who you was?"

"Why didn't you ask? But even without asking, you were going to sell me the Hawken that my pa already paid for and the pistol too!"

"But, but, I didn't know!" protested the trader.

"Never mind, just hand me a couple of those feed sacks and help me pack this stuff out to my horse," ordered Tatum, disgusted with another example of mankind.

With the feed sacks tied together and behind the cantle of the saddle, Tatum stepped aboard and rested the Hawken across the pommel and put the pistol into his waistband. He nodded to Blue and reined his horse around to return to his cabin. The rest of the afternoon was spent sorting out his supplies and packing things into the panniers for the pack saddle. He put the cooking gear, pans, plates, cups and utensils in on top of some of the foodstuffs and the other pannier held a few clothing items, some books chosen at random from his father's library, blankets and extra shooting supplies with the rest of the food items. He reserved the saddle bags for things needed at the ready like extra powder, caps, bandages and ointments which he hoped he wouldn't need, and other everyday items. He made up a bedroll with a couple of blankets and an extra shirt and a groundcover. As he thought of other things, he found a place either in the panniers, the parfleche that would ride atop the panniers, or the saddle bags.

Before dusk, Tatum went into the clearing and set up a couple of boards with an "X" marked in charcoal for targets. He thought he should at least try out the new weapons before he started on the trip. After all, you never know when you'll need to put them to use and it would pay to know how to use them. He was used to his New Bedford flintlock but calculated the Hawken would need a bit more powder and he measured out twice the amount he used for the flinter with the small cap from the powder horn. He laid the patch atop the muzzle, pushed the ball down into the muzzle with the ball starter, and finished the job with the ramrod, seating the ball against the powder. He brought the rifle up to his chest, cocked the hammer to seat the percussion cap, lifted the rifle to his shoulder, steadied it on the target, slowly pulled the set trigger back to the click and brought his finger to the front trigger. He put the front blade sight at the cross mark, lined it up with the buckhorn sight on the rear, took a breath, let part of it out and slowly squeezed the trigger. The big

Hawken bucked in his hands, rocked him back on his heels, rammed against his shoulder and with a roar and a small cloud of blue-grey smoke, sent the .54 caliber ball toward its mark. Upon impact, the ball split the board in two and continued into the stump behind.

"Whoooeee!" proclaimed an excited Tatum. "That's a rifle!"

He spent the next hour experimenting with both the Hawken and the Paterson and by the time dusk had swapped places with darkness, he felt confident with both weapons. He knew it would take some time and considerable experience before his confidence would become competence but he was happy with his ability to use both the rifle and pistol. He knew he would need a good night's rest before starting his journey on the morrow so he begrudgingly put the firearms aside and turned in for the night.

By first light, Tatum was saddling his sorrel and the big bay that had been his father's. The bay shied away from the pack saddle at first but soon settled down and succumbed to Tatum's ministrations and packing with the panniers and parfleche. He secured his longbow and quiver atop the pannier and beside the parfleche. He made a last pass through the cabin and the shed, found a couple of hand tools he missed and slipped them into the near side pannier. With a last look around, he tipped his hat to his father's grave with the spade still serving as a marker, said, "G'bye, Pa," and reined his mount around and started on the trail to the Tallchief home.

As he neared the cabin of his friends, he saw they were seated on the porch as if awaiting his arrival. They waved as he approached and he stepped down and tethered the horses at the rail in front of the cabin. He mounted the steps with a long face looking at his friends. Jeremiah Tallchief stood and reached out to shake the young man's hand. Sacred Sun,

Tallchief's wife, held her arms wide to give Tatum a motherly hug. She held him tight and spoke in his ear, "I have something for you." She pulled back at arm's length and looked at the young man, saw the grief behind the mask of a smile, then reached down to the chairs and handed a bundle to Tatum. She smiled at him and said, "That's another set of buckskins for you. I didn't have time to do much beading but there is a colorful row of quills that were sewn with love so you will remember us."

Tatum accepted the bundle and looked to Sacred Sun with tears welling up again, and said, "I'm very grateful; I didn't mean for Red Calf to get you to do that. I left some hides in the shed for you and anything else you want."

She pointed to the bundle and said, "Those are the hides from your shed. Red Calf brought them to me yesterday." She smiled at his surprise and hugged him again. He turned to Tallchief and said, "I will forever be in your debt for all you taught me. I wouldn't feel confident about going, save for the knowledge you shared with me, and I thank you."

"Knowledge is for sharing, that's how we all learn. And you have taught us about friendship and loyalty. Thank you," responded Tallchief.

Red Calf had been standing to the side while his parents spoke to his friend but now stepped forward and said, "I will ride with you a way, then we will say our good-byes."

Sacred Sun hugged Tatum once more and the young man clasped forearms with Tallchief before stepping from the porch and mounting up to leave. Red Calf came from behind the cabin astride his blue roan gelding and came alongside his friend as they both took to the trail that led to the west toward what had become known as Indian Territory with the Indian Removal Act of 1830. But Tatum would take the fork in the trail that would lead him into unorganized territory and through the northern part of Indian Territory. It was at that fork the friends reined up and said their good-byes. With clasped arms and few words, Tatum handed his flintlock rifle to Red Calf and said, "That was my pa's and I'm sure he'd want you to have it." Red Calf looked at the rifle, smiled at his friend and they parted with Tatum watching his friend disappear into the thick woods that shrouded the return trail. He lifted his head, reined his mount around, tugged at the lead rope of the packhorse and said, "Let's go to the mountains!"

CHAPTER FIVE
BEGINNING

TATUM WAS DETERMINED TO MAKE HIS PASSAGE AS inconspicuous as possible. In his present state of mind, he did not want to be around people any more than was necessary and he also knew that a young man traveling alone could be considered a target for any number of highwaymen or unfriendly Indians. His father had told him about a recently built military outpost named Fort Scott that was just over the border of Missouri territory and in the northern portion of Indian territory. The road to Fort Scott was new but well-traveled, although Tatum had yet to see any travelers and he was nearing the end of his third day on the trail. Each evening he had been careful in selecting his campsite, always moving from the roadway into an area with water and graze for the horses, well protected with ample trees for cover. The end of this day's travel provided a good site that met all his needs and he made himself a comfortable camp. A small campfire from dry wood gave little smoke and he usually put the fire out before full dark.

The long shadows from the towering oak and elm stretched across the smoldering coals as he sat with his back to a log and feet towards the fire. He heard a hail from a voice in the direction of the roadway that was forty yards distant, "Halloo the camp! I'm peaceable; can I come in?" The voice sounded scratchy and Tatum jumped to his feet then knelt behind the stump end of the log and answered, "Come on but keep your hands high." He watched as a grizzled old man tottered into the clearing, his hands over his head and holding a Kentucky-style rifle. Attired in dark buckskins, he had a full face of grey whiskers and some kind of fur cap that had the face of a small animal to the front. His eyes sparkled and what would pass for a smile parted the whiskers and showed a few brown teeth. Tatum noted the ample beadwork across the chest of his buckskin shirt and matching beadwork down the sleeves and on the toes of his moccasins. Tattered fringe also crossed his chest and down his sleeves and trouser legs as well. To Tatum, he was the picture of the storied mountain men he had heard about. Tatum held the Paterson Colt level with his waist and directed at the man as he showed himself beside the rooted stump of the log. "Go ahead and have a seat. If you got a cup, there's coffee."

"Wal, thankee friend, thankee. It's been a spell since I run out o' coffee and it shore smells fine." He was bow-legged but still agile and stepped across the opposite log, laid his rifle against it, and dropped a pack from his back and retrieved a cup. As he bent to pour himself some java, Tatum stepped over his log and sat on it with the Paterson hanging between his knees. As the old man seated himself, he looked at Tatum, grinned and said, "Why, yore a young un' ain'tcha? Oh, by the way, my name's Rastus an' I'm on my way to visit muh famly' in Cape Girardeau. Ever been there?"

"Yup, used to live there a spell," answered Tatum, not volunteering any additional information.

Rastus motioned with his cup toward Tatum and said,

"Yore right to be careful, young'un. Cain't never tell whatchu might run into. Have you got a handle?"

"Name's Tatum, or Tate."

"Well, Tate, how come a young'un like you's out here by yoreself?"

"What makes you think I'm by myself?"

The old timer chuckled and said, "Son, I been through the woods an' oer the mountain more times than you've been to the outhouse, an' you ain't gonna pull the wool oer this ol' man's eyes. Ya see, there's only one set o' tracks around this hyar camp, only one bedroll," and nodded at the bedroll away from the fire. "And even though you got two horses, I can see by the packs yonder, yore ridin' one and packin' th' other'n. Now, don't go gittin' skittish on me; I don't mean ya no harm, just lookin' ta' share yore fire and yore coffee. So, rest easy, an' let's jabber a bit."

Tatum looked at the old-timer and tried to read his expression as his father had often taught him; he saw nothing to be alarmed about but still chose to be cautious. He sat the Colt on the log beside him but within easy reach and turned to Rastus and asked, "To look at you, I'd say you came from the mountains, am I right?"

The whiskered face showed a grin and he answered, "That's right, from the Rocky Mountains or the far blue mountains as some call 'em. God's country! Spent most o' the last forty years thar and I seen ever'thin' and done ever'thin', yessireebob."

"So, were you a trapper?"

"Certain sure, I was. I done it with the best of 'em. Bridger, Carson, Provost, Johnson, Meek, Smith, yup, knowed 'em all. Course, ol' Colter and Drouillard and even ol' Manuel Lisa were all there 'fore I was. Great country, that. Hate to leave it but muh ol' bones just cain't take the cold no more, no sir." He looked at the young man across the fire ring and asked, "It that what'chur plannin' on? Trappin'?"

"No, I'm just goin' to the mountains to get away from all these people," and motioned with a sweep of his hand. "It was somethin' me and my Pa always talked about so . . ." and he let his gaze drop to the few smoldering coals. The old-timer looked at the forlorn expression on the boy's face and knew he had something weighing on him, maybe a loss of some kind.

He lowered his voice a bit and asked Tatum, "Just lost yore pa, didja?"

Tatum looked up at the old-timer and nodded his head without answering.

"Wal son, I wisht I was goin' wit'chu. I was 'bout yore age when I went to the mountains an' I can say yore in for quite an adventure, yessir, quite an adventure. Why, I remember my first time seein' them mountains, never thot anything could be so purty an' so big. Why them granite peaks seem to reach right up an' scratch the blue of the sky." He paused as his memory took hold and he looked into the past, then continued, "Why, them mountains got big ol' elk, Grizzly bear bigger'n a horse, two horses, long-tailed cougars, wolves that'll cry you to sleep, and anything else you want to eat, shoot, or ride. And that ain't even sayin' nuthin' 'bout them wooly boogers, them buffler. Yessir, that's God's country alright."

They talked well into the night, letting the crescent moon and starlight set the mood of discovery and learning and sharing. The old man willingly answered all the questions that came from the eager young man and he was quick to demonstrate anything that aided the learning of the anxious student. Yet both young and old gave in to the late hour and turned to their bedrolls for the night.

Tatum was still in his blankets when the old-timer moved

toward the sleeping form. He reached out with the barrel of his long-rifle and tapped the foot of the boy. Tatum lifted his head to look at the man that stood to the side, grinning at the youngster. "See thar, even after you did like I said an' scattered them twigs and leaves aroun', I was still able to catch you sleepin'."

Tatum grinned and said, "Didju?" and flipped the edge of his blanket back to reveal the Paterson Colt in his hand and trained on the chest of the old-timer. The whiskered old man laughed and stepped back and said, "Good one, yessir, you'll do to ride the river with, yessir." He turned away and Tatum saw the old man had his pack on and was ready to leave. The boy stood up and asked, "You leavin'? Without havin' coffee?"

"Oh, I had the rest of the coffee from last night. After sittin' near them coals all night, it was just 'bout thick 'nuff for me. And yes, I'm leavin'. I got a long way to go an' I wanna git thar 'fore I die, an' the rate I'm goin' I might not make it."

Tatum reached out to shake the hand of the old-timer and said, "Thanks for tellin' me all that stuff last night. I appreciate it."

"Shore, shore, you just make shore you never quit larnin' cuz it'll take ever'thin' you got, an' sometimes more, for you to survive in them mountains. They're beeeutiful but they can be deadly, too, an' don't forget that!" and nodded his head vigorously to emphasize his point.

"I will, I will. And you go with God."

Rastus looked at him and said, "Son, God is always with me, always has been and always will be. You just listen to yore own preachin' now, hear? An' as we say in the mountains, keep yore topknot on!"

Tatum smiled and nodded his head in understanding and lifted his hand to wave to the one white man, other than his father, that he respected. He looked around his camp and turned to get the horses from the picket line and began packing up for the day's journey. He had discussed the route with Rastus and the old-timer confirmed his plans of going to Fort Scott, then making his way due west across the flats until he came to the Sante Fe Trail at the Arkansas River, and then follow the river to the mountains. Sounded simple enough but he knew the journey would take at least a month, probably more, just to make it to the mountains and then, well, that would be decided after he got there.

THE SOLITUDE OF THE TRAIL GAVE TATUM AMPLE TIME FOR reflection and contemplation. He knew the path he was following had been used many times before during the forced relocation of the many Indian peoples from east of the Mississippi and other lands that the ever-expanding hordes of white settlers wanted for their farm plows. He remembered his father telling about the tribulations of the Cherokee people that were forced from their homes in Georgia and made to travel over 1,000 miles carrying all they owned and often traveling without ample clothing and bare-foot. He said the Cherokee called it the *nu na hi du na tlo hi lu i* or the *Trail Where They Cried.* Tatum shook his head at the remembrance and reminder of the cruelty of man, and thought how everywhere he went he saw repeated examples of mankind's evil. He thought, *God, I don't know why you put up with it. If I were you, I think I'd have to kill 'em all!*

The click of his horse's hoof on a stone brought him from his reverie and he looked up to see the trail leading from the woods into a wide expanse of grassland. As he came to the edge of the trees, he reined up and leaned forward, resting his crossed forearms on the saddle horn and looked at a scene that filled him with an awe never before felt. The canopy of blue seemed to stretch into infinity and the waving grasses, belly-deep on a tall horse, beckoned him into the sunlight. He sat up, took a deep breath that lifted his shoulders and spread the smile on his face from ear to ear, and clucked his horse forward. The sun bathed him in warmth and he pulled the brim of his floppy felt hat down to shade his eyes.

He had never seen such an expanse of land. He thought it was like the ocean that his father spoke of but this was a vast panorama of rolling hills covered with tall grass that moved with the wind like the waves on a lake or, as his father had described, the waves on an ocean. He stood in his stirrups and scanned the entire horizon—north, west, and south—and as far as he could see, the grassy waves seemed to sing a song of freedom to his anxious ears and eyes. He shouted, "Whoooeeee!" and the sudden noise startled his horse that kicked out like he'd been smacked on the rump, then ducked his head between his feet and started crow hopping as Tatum tugged on the reins to pull his head up. The sudden explosion of energy from the boy and his horse also startled the packhorse who jerked the lead rope from Tatum's hands, now busy with trying to stay aboard his mount, and skittered away.

Tatum got his mount settled down, leaned down to give a reassuring pat on the side of his neck, and looked around for the packhorse. Fortunately, the big bay was more interested in the taste of this new grass than he was in exploring new territory and was standing a short distance away, cropping his morning snack. He lifted his head at the whistle of Tatum, the sound he usually heard when the young man was coming to feed him, and trotted over to his traveling companions and waited for Tatum to take the lead rope that was trailing behind. "That's a good boy. Sure glad you didn't take off too far. That crazy kid makin' all that noise was enough to scare the beegeebers out of anything, wasn't it, boy?" He reached down and grabbed the lead rope, pulled on it and realized the bay was standing on the end of the rope. But with a gentle tug, the big bay stepped forward allowing Tatum to pull the rope up and dally it around the horn.

Tatum looked at the sun and at the shadows beneath the horses and figured it to be nearing mid-day. The trail led away to the west-northwest and following the trail with his eyes, he saw some buildings on a distant bluff. "Well boys," speaking to his only companions, the horses, "I make that out to be Fort Scott. But since we're purty well supplied, I ain't interested in goin' there so how 'bout we just head straight west from here? Hummm, I think we'll make for that patch o' dark green yonder; that's probly' some trees and maybe some water 'n that'd be a good place fer our noonin', what say?" The only response he got from his traveling companions was the flick of an ear and a slight head toss from the sorrel. He put his heels to his mount and they started for the distant landmark.

His father had taken every opportunity to teach his son— whether in the woods about animals, survival and path-finding or in their home or classroom about the way of the world. But the lessons learned in the hardwood forests of Missouri were not applicable to the plains. Now he had to rely on his own ingenuity using the position of the sun for direc-tion and, traveling in unfamiliar country, landmarks were unknown. But the freedom to explore and learn more than made up for his previous reliance on old lessons. The patch of dark green turned out to be the treetops of a cluster of cotton-wood that lined the bank of a narrow creek in the bottom of a wide ravine where Tatum now sat leaning against the taller of the trees and watching his horses graze at the end of their picketed lead ropes. He chewed on some of the venison jerky he and his father smoked the week before his death.

As he watched the horses, he thought about the trail ahead. He thought about what Rastus had told him of different Indian tribes he may encounter. He knew he was in Osage country but he thought of the Osage as a friendly people, thinking of Red Calf and his family. But his father had often warned him, "Just because someone's friendly, doesn't mean his family or friends will be friendly, so always be on your guard." Even Tallchief had explained to him about some of his own people resenting the encroaching white settlers and how the Osage had been a tribe of warriors that were known for their fierce fighting ways.

He stood and looked around, stepped across the small creek and climbed up the opposite bluff of the ravine. As he stood on the rim of the bluff, he shaded his eyes and looked to the west for any sign of concern. Stretching out before him was the endless expanse of grassy flatlands, deceptive in its appearance for Tatum had already observed the many dips and ravines and arroyos that marked what otherwise looked like unmarred flatlands. He looked up at the position of the sun, guesstimated the time left in the day and, looking back at the horses and the area below, made his decision. *Yup, I'm gonna stay here, get me some sleep, have my supper and start travelin' at night. Should be a lot safer, 'specially in Indian country.* Then he realized he would probably be in Indian country from now on, the only difference being which Indians, and chuckled to himself.

The night had dropped its mantle of darkness and pulled back the curtain of diamonds to decorate the biggest sky Tatum ever scanned. *Wow! It looks like I could just reach up and touch 'em, they're so close!* He had just topped out from the ravine and now sat astride his sorrel with the big bay in tow as he searched the heavens for the constellation his father called *Ursa Minor.* He remembered the times his father used the stars to tell about the ancient astrologists and the constellations. *Ursa Minor* was also known as the bear and he knew the tail, even though bears didn't have tails, was tipped by the North Star which would be his night guide across the Great Plains. *There!* He pointed it out and holding his arm extended, he looked ahead at the moonlit landscape and started out, glancing back at the star to keep it just off his right shoulder.

His first night traveling under the stars was without incident but not without wonder. The big moon was a comforting companion as Tatum's eyes grew accustomed to the vastness of the flatlands. Although the occasional ravine or arroyo with small creeks or clusters of alder or willow provided challenging interludes, the night travel was comforting and reassuring. But the darkness that hid his passing could also be used as a cloak for dangers and Tatum stayed vigilant. As the stars began to dim their brilliance and the moon followed the path of the previous day's sun, Tatum searched for a campsite for his day's rest.

The sorrel pulled up and brought his rider's attention forward to see a significant drop-off no more than a couple of paces in front of his horse. He leaned forward along the neck of the sorrel and saw a blackness that indicated a steep bank into a deep ravine. He stepped down and walked to the edge, peered over and let his eyes become familiar with the darkness, and saw a thick patch of cottonwood and willow in the bottom of a steep-sided ravine. He looked left and right for a possible way into the ravine, spotted a slope to his left and led his horses behind him to investigate. It was a lesser gradient and he led his mounts down into what would be his first daylight camp. A small creek was sided by willows and a suitable grassy clearing that he thought would be acceptable for their camp.

He unsaddled the mounts, dropped the packs and gear near the trees, tethered the horses and began preparing his breakfast.

He built a small fire near the trees to let the overhanging branches filter the smoke, put on the coffee and a pan of salt pork to go with the leftover corn biscuits. After his filling breakfast, he eagerly went to his blankets for his much-anticipated rest. As he stretched out and looked at the slowly greying sky, he smiled to himself and thought, *Yeah, it's been a good night's travel. Good thinkin', Tatum, good thinkin',* and let sleep overtake him.

CHAPTER SEVEN
INDIANS

TATUM HAD LONG BEEN A LIGHT SLEEPER, HIS RESTLESSNESS starting when his mother took sick and he had been tasked with tending to her during the early morning hours. Afraid she would wake and need something and he didn't hear her, he listened and dozed but never into a deep sleep. And after his Mother died and his father turned to drink, he would sleep light waiting for his father to return home. He subconsciously trained himself to be attentive even when sleeping. That practice had served him well on the trail and brought him to full wakefulness late in his first afternoon of night travel. The low rumble and shuffling from atop the ridge was something he hadn't heard before and he slipped from his covers, grabbing his Hawken, possibles bag and powder horn, and cautiously worked his way up the bank toward the sound. Before cresting the ridge, he saw dust rising and heard a shuffling low rumble that made him think of a coming thunderstorm, but different. As he lifted his head over the edge, he was startled at his first sight of a buffalo herd. The big wooly beasts were moving slowly along the edge of the ravine.

Tatum watched as cows paused to let their orange furred calves push against their bags and nurse while they cropped grass. As he watched, farther out a big bull was pawing at the dirt then lay down to roll, stirring up the dust. Others swung their ponderous heads and let low moans rumble from deep in their bellies as they looked for their next mouthful of grass. It was a family scene and Tatum grinned at the sight. *Boy, Rastus wasn't kidding when he said these things are big!* He continued to watch the shuffling herd, enjoying the scene of his newfound countryside, the land of wide open vistas and amazing discoveries.

Suddenly several of the buffalo lifted their heads and looked in the same direction, then turned and started to run. Tatum heard the screams of pursuing Indians as several mounted warriors started their hunt for buffalo. The mounted hunters gave chase as they attacked the flanks of the rumbling herd; a few of the warriors had trade fusils and fired them one handed as they rode alongside the brown beasts. Others were wielding lances or bows as they too rode among the thundering mass. Tatum stood to see the hunters better and was amazed at the horsemanship of several of them that would ride within scant inches of a massive beast and needing both hands for their bows and arrows, held tight to their mounts with only their legs. Tatum knew if a horse were to stumble, the rider would be crushed by the stampeding buffalo, each one weighing at least half a ton and more. Yet the warriors would repeatedly shoot arrows into the side or neck of the buffalo before the prey would stumble and often somersault head over heels. Then the warrior would continue his hunt, pursuing his next target. It was a thrilling sight and Tatum was mesmerized by the scene before him.

Suddenly, a warrior's horse stumbled and Tatum saw the Indian fly over the horse's head and land in a heap just past the downed horse. He scrambled to his feet and used the horse as cover but much of the herd was still behind them and charging in his direction. Tatum looked to see a large number headed directly toward the hunter and he quickly lifted his Hawken, sighted swiftly, set the trigger and squeezed off the shot. He aimed for the heart, directly behind the foreleg and low on the chest, and the bull stumbled, dropped his head and skidded on his chin in the dirt causing the animals behind him to veer to the side. Tatum quickly reloaded, all the while watching the charging herd and the downed warrior. When he lowered the Hawken for another shot, he saw the herd had thinned out and was moving on to the south. Tatum looked at the warrior, saw he was safe, and relieved, he dropped below the edge of the ravine to break camp.

He hurriedly saddled up, did his best to cover any sign of a camp, and started down the ravine. He knew he would have to circumvent the area of the buffalo hunt and chose to move to the north and then resume his westward trek. He had ridden less than a hundred yards when he saw three warriors ride to the edge of the ravine and look down at him. He immediately recognized them as Osage, seeing their size and scalp-locks. The traditional Osage would carefully remove all facial hair, including their eyebrows and much of their hair, leaving a standing tuft from the center to the neckline and often have a small braid that would hang down the back. Sometimes they would decorate their hair with feathers or other colorful bits of cloth or leather. Many would cut their ears and dangle decorative carvings from them, and tattoo themselves or wear many beads or other decorative items. But the most distinguishing feature was their height, most men well over six feet.

When he saw them, he reined up and lifted his hand with open palm forward and nodded his head to them. They paused just a moment and started down the slope to intercept him. Tatum did not speak their language but the apparent leader of the trio spoke to him saying simply, "Come." Tatum looked at him and at the stern faces of the others, nodded his head and followed them back up the slope to the flats now covered with many carcasses with women and a few men busy with the skinning and butchering.

With the one warrior in front, followed by Tatum astride his sorrel and leading his packhorse, and two warriors behind, they rode to the downed warrior Tatum had seen earlier who now sat on the carcass of his horse and was being tended to by a woman. He looked up at their arrival, lifted a hand in greeting and spoke to Tatum, "I want to thank you for what you did," motioning to the carcass of the bull buffalo less than thirty feet distant. Tatum looked at the bull and back at the man and said, "You're welcome."

The warrior looked past Tatum and at the others then spoke again to Tatum and said, "You are traveling alone?"

"Yes," answered Tatum without explanation.

"Then you will join us as we celebrate our successful hunt," he stated as he waved his arm around to indicate the many downed buffalo. "You will share in our feast and you will take your kill," motioning to the downed bull.

Tatum looked at the big bull carcass and said, "I can't carry that much meat but I will be glad to join you for a meal. Have your people take this and share it among them as my gift."

The warrior grinned and said, "You are generous, and how are you called?"

"Tatum, Tatum Saint."

"It is good, Tatum Tatum Saint, and I am Black Buffalo and these are my people." Motioning with another sweeping gesture, he said, "We are the *Ni-u-kon-ska* or as some would say *Wazhazhe.* Step down and join me. The women will prepare the feast soon and we will have much to eat."

Tatum soon learned that Black Buffalo was one of the leaders of the Osage and wanted to show his appreciation for Tatum killing the bull that would have trampled the downed warrior. Black Buffalo asked the young man what he might need for his journey and Tatum was at a loss to tell him of anything he would need or wanted, believing himself to be well outfitted. Yet for the remainder of the evening and during the meal, Tatum noticed Black Buffalo always visually searching him and his gear for some idea of what he could give this young traveler to pay his debt. Because of Black Buffalo's status within the ranks of the Osage, the women had prepared the feast near where he sat with his visitor and the men were seated near the cook fire while they talked.

It was well into the night when Tatum rose and said to his host, "Black Buffalo, I am grateful for the meal and your company. It was a pleasure getting to know you and your people but I must be going."

The leader looked up at the young man, rose to his feet to stand beside him and asked, "You are going to travel at night?"

"Yup, I kinda like ridin' in the moonlight." Motioning to the slow rising bright shining full moon to the east, he said, "It's plumb peaceful and 'sides, the coyotes sing to me all the way." He grinned at his new friend and reached out to clasp hands. The warrior grinned back, thinking how this young man's heart was so much like his, and motioned to a woman nearby. As he clasped forearms with his visitor, the woman came beside him and handed him a bundle. He passed the bundle to Tatum and said, "This is for the cool nights as you ride and think of my people and this time we shared whenever you look upon it."

"Why, thank you, Black Buffalo. I will always remember

this time and your fine people and should our paths ever cross again, may we once again enjoy our time together." He turned to mount up, a warrior having fetched his horses for him, and swung aboard, nodded at his new friend and pointed his mount's head to the west and dug heels. The clear night and star-studded sky urged him onward and he heard the cry of a distant coyote that was answered by another, and smiled as he faced the unknown plains before him.

CHAPTER EIGHT
PLAINS

TATUM'S NIGHT-TIME TRAVEL HAD SERVED HIM WELL BUT THE moon was waning to its last quarter and even though the nights had been clear, the star light wasn't enough to let Tatum spot any perils in their chosen path of travel. He had also exhausted his meat supply, having consumed the last of the buffalo the morning meal of the day yesterday. He knew he would need to do some hunting to replenish his supply and planned on an early morning hunt when he stopped. A mild breeze blew against his face and he caught a hint of smoke causing him to rein up and survey the area. The darkness prevented him seeing anything alarming but he was certain of what he smelled and continued searching the darkness for any sign of a campfire. Nothing. He stepped to the ground and with his rifle at the ready, he looped the rein over his arm and started forward. The black shadows before him told of trees and brush and he slowly approached.

Tatum had continually practiced his stealth from the time of his early instructions at his father's side when they stalked deer in the forest and when he hunted with his Osage friend, Red Calf, and that practice again served him well. He dropped the reins to ground tie his horse and moved forward in a crouch. The trees and brush were in a slight dip of a creek bottom and Tatum found cover behind some sage. He looked to the trees and searched for any sign of movement but there was none. But as he watched, he saw a spark rise from some ash-covered coals of a campfire. He continued to examine the scene before him and began to make out a single tethered horse, three or four forms near the fire, and a stack of gear near a tree. There was nothing that would easily identify the group, but Tatum sensed more than knew that these were Indians. He hadn't seen any whites since his visit with the Osage but that had been three days past and this camp had no saddles or other accouterments usual for a white man's camp.

Tatum backed away from the brush and returned to his horses. He mounted up and circled wide around the sleeping forms to continue on to find himself a camp. He was tired from traveling several days without an extended stop and was looking forward to getting fresh meat and maybe spend a day or more letting his horses and himself get some needed rest. Less than two miles further he came to a likely looking spot for a camp. Good trees—willows—a stream, and situated in a long arroyo that would be good cover, Tatum smiled as he reined his mount toward the trees. He made camp, tethered the horses, and taking his long bow, started down along the stream searching for game trails in the grey light before dawn. He looked back along his trail and smiled at the band of pink that signaled the start of another day; this would be the best time for a hunt, what with deer coming to the stream for their first drink of the day.

He soon sighted a trail leading from the rise in the east and down to the stream. He looked to his left, spotted a cluster of willows and stepped behind them for cover enabling him to watch the trail and the clearing to the creek.

He had little time to wait before he spotted the shadowy figure of a small buck warily walking down the trail toward the stream. He had already nocked an arrow but waited until the deer was broadside and focused on the stream before he stepped from behind the bush and stepped into his bow, releasing the arrow. The shaft whispered true to its aim and buried itself in the neck of the buck who stumbled and, as its knees buckled, dropped forward. Tatum started forward as he reached for his sheathed Bowie knife, another recent purchase of his father's, to bleed the buck. He knelt beside the carcass, laid his bow aside, and reached forward to slit the throat of the buck but was stopped when he heard a step just beyond the deer. He looked up to see an Indian with a bow and nocked arrow pointing at him and motioning toward the buck. Tatum looked at the man and asked, "What?" as the Indian again motioned at Tatum as if ordering him away from the deer. Tatum looked at the man and again at the buck, then noticed his arrow had completely pene-trated the neck of the animal with only the fletching protruding. But on the other side and just behind the shoul-der, another arrow protruded. He reached toward the arrow, noted the decorated shaft and fletching, then turned back to the bow holding warrior and said, "Look here," and motioned to his arrow in the neck, "looks like we both shot the same deer." He waved at the man to come closer and pointed at the two arrows. The warrior slowly approached, saw what the white man was pointing at and nodded his head but, with a scowl, motioned for Tatum to move away. Tatum looked at him and shook his head, then asked, "I guess you don't understand English, huh? Okay, let's try this," and began motioning to the deer. Using his knife, he indicated he would take one hindquarter and the warrior could take the rest. When the Indian didn't make any other moves either of understanding or threatening, he began cutting.

He split the deer from throat to tail, removed the entrails, then cut away around the left hindquarter. When he sat his share aside, he stood up and backed away from the carcass. He motioned to the Indian that what remained was his, then bent down and picked up his bow, grabbed the quarter and turned his back to the man and walked away. It wasn't until he was well away from the carcass that he looked back and saw the man eagerly finishing with the butchering of the deer. Tatum smiled and continued to his camp.

He built a small fire, using only dry wood and positioning the fire so the smoke would dissipate easily, and sliced off a good-sized steak for his breakfast. He hung the steak over the flames on a green willow branch and let the juices drip into the fire. While he waited for the steak to cook, he set a batch of cornbread biscuits to baking in his Dutch oven that sat on a batch of coals and with more on the lid. He then started slicing the fresh haunch of venison into thin strips to smoke into jerky but because the smoking required greener wood like the nearby alders, it would have to wait until after dark when the smoke wouldn't show.

He thought about his recent visit with the Osage and wondered if the camp he'd seen was a family from the Osage but then thought of the warrior at the deer and realized he was not Osage but some other tribe. He'd heard that this was Kansa territory and that some of the displaced Cherokee were known to be in this area, but he didn't know what tribe the warrior was from or how to distinguish the difference. He thought the Osage were easily identified by their hair and height but he knew little of the uniqueness of the other tribes. Thinking about the Osage, he remembered the bundle that Black Buffalo had given him and realized he hadn't opened it to see what it was, having stuffed it into the far pannier and forgotten about it. He rose from his seat and went to the pannier to retrieve the parcel.

He sat back down near the fire and began to undo the parcel. Whatever it was it was made of soft tanned buckskin and as he unfolded it, he saw a decorative band of bead work combined with muted colored quill work. As he started to hold it up, a heavy object fell beside his foot. He reached down and brought up a magnificent tomahawk with a metal head that had the bowl of a pipe opposite the blade of two colors of metal. Finely crafted, he knew this had been an expensive object of trade but the handle had been carved and decorated by the Osage. Although hollowed out so it could be used as a pipe, the hardwood appeared to be cedar and was exquisitely carved with the outstretched wings of an eagle extending the length of the handle. Near the head, a wide band of beadwork gave additional color to the weapon. Tatum looked and turned it around and over to examine every portion, shaking his head at the wonderful craftsmanship, knowing this was an exceptional gift. Then he remembered the buckskin and, setting the tomahawk aside, he lifted the buckskin bundle to hold at arm's length and caught his breath at the beautiful beaded and fringed coat. It was lined with white rabbit fur and was as impressive as the tomahawk for its beauty and craftsmanship. He turned it around and saw the back yoke was also decorated with beads and quills in a starburst design of multiple colors. He stood and slipped it on but it was a little big for him. Yet he knew he would grow into it soon enough and, until then, he could still wear it if need be; he felt the softness of the leather while he pulled it off to set it aside. He shook his head in wonder at the beautiful gifts before him and said, "Thank you, Black Buffalo," and lifting his head upward added, "And thank you God for your many blessings and making this journey safe and for the friends you've brought across my path. Thank you."

CHAPTER NINE
PRAIRIE

EVERYONE ENJOYED THE FEW DAYS OF REST, HORSES AND MAN alike, and all were ready to hit the trail again. The few days gave Tatum the time and opportunity to increase his larder with smoked venison and enjoy several fresh steaks broiled over the campfire. The animals had repeatedly eaten their fill of the lush grasses and were beginning to get a mite lazy. But Tatum knew time on the trail would soon get them back in traveling shape. The days of peace and quiet had refreshed the young man and his eagerness to see the Rockies was renewed. As darkness settled over the flats, Tatum waited until the waxing moon showed its first quarter and the stars glowed in all their brilliance. With his eyes now accustomed to the dark, he mounted up and started afresh on his trail west.

The terrain gradually changed from broad flat grasslands to prairie with scattered clumps of sage, tufts of buffalo grass and grama, thickets of scrub brush and patches of many different types of cacti. With dry ravines holding rocky banks and rolling hills that often rose to rimrock-topped mesas, it became more difficult for the travelers to maintain a direct west route. The chosen path resembled the trail of a serpent more than the flight of an eagle.

Tatum continued to navigate by the stars and became more habituated to the dark and felt himself becoming a nocturnal traveler and enjoying the journey in the dim light. He listened for the love songs of the coyote, the rattling whisper of the cicada, the lonesome questions of the owls and even the plaintive screams of the occasional desert cougar. But his favorite of all were the rare howls of the wolves, never to be heard in solo but always in concert with those scattered across the prairie and nearly invisible to the usual traveler.

It was almost a week before Tatum needed to hunt again and with the moon waxing to full, he wanted to make his hunt, get the day's rest, and continue without delay. Well before dawn overtook them, he found a sandy-bottomed arroyo with a trickle of a stream that would be adequate for their water and the steep rocky bank on the far side gave sufficient cover. A cluster of juniper fronted the rocky bank and gave additional cover and sheltered a patch of grass to refresh the animals. After derigging, he picketed the horses within reach of the water and grass, stacked the gear by the bluff and, with longbow in hand, started his hunt.

He moved upstream from his campsite, staying in the arroyo and the source of water for the animals of the prairie. He was mastering his stealth and moved silently on the sandy creek bottom, weaving in and out of the scattered brush and trees. As the sunrise painted the wispy clouds overhead, he spotted movement and froze behind a clump of willow. He slowly moved to get a better view and had his first sighting of antelope. One nice-sized buck was pushing three doe and their fawns to the water. His black pronghorns were occasionally used to urge the last doe forward but he often lifted his head to scan the area for danger. Tatum was too far away and there was too much brush between him and the antelope to risk a shot. He watched and waited for the buck to look away and each time the buck turned his head, Tatum moved closer. Finally, when he thought he was near enough, he readied himself for a shot. He nocked an arrow and started his draw but the longbow required more than a simple arm-strength draw; he had to step into the pull utilizing the strength of both arms and the upper body as well. When the buck lowered his head to drink, Tatum stood and started his draw. But the keen hearing and eyesight of the antelope gave alarm and as one they jumped; in two leaps they crossed the small stream and ran up the bank to disappear over the edge. Tatum's arrow was mostly buried in the sand beyond the slight game trail and he ran to retrieve the arrow before mounting the bank to see if he had another shot. When he crested the bank, all he saw was the bouncing white rumps of antelope well over two hundred yards distant and well beyond range of the longbow.

Tatum replaced the arrow in his quiver, shook his head and chuckled to himself as he thought, *I ain't never seen anything move so fast! They were somethin' alright. Guess I'll have to be smarter next time.* As he shuffled through the sand on his way back to his camp, he jumped a big jackrabbit from the willows and his quick reaction netted him a tasty bit of fresh meat for breakfast.

His bedroll had him stretched out in the shade of the junipers and on the opposite side from the picketed horses. The late afternoon sun tried in vain to reach the sleeping form well-hidden beneath the low branches of the spreading juniper, but a shuffling noise stirred him from his sleep. He awoke just in time to see two Indian boys grab the manes and swing up on the horses, kick them furiously and horses and riders crashed from the trees. Tatum came up from his blankets to a seated position with the Hawken to his shoulder and fired towards the fleeing horse thieves, the recoil of the Hawken knocking him flat on his back. The big bay, always one that hated the sound of gunshots, exploded under his youthful rider. He tucked his head between his hoofs and kicked his hind legs at the sunset. He stretched out so far one would think he was trying to kick the sun back into yesterday and launch himself into next week. He screamed an ear-splitting whinny and reared up to paw at the single cloud that hovered in the azure sky. Switching ends in mid-flight, he loosed his rider from his frantic grip of the mane and disappeared from under the falling figure. Although the sorrel wasn't gun-shy, when he saw his traveling companion take flight, it seemed like the thing to do and he quickly followed suit. But the sorrel wasn't as rank as the big bay and even though he sun-fished, showed his belly to the sun, the young rider hung on for dear life. But the sorrel stumbled, went down on his knees and started to roll causing the young Indian to jump free of this crazy horse.

By now, Tatum was standing bare-chested and in his holey stockings, watching the antics of his usually docile animals and chuckled at the dismay shown on the faces of the would-be horse thieves. Once free of their riders, the horses sidled up to each other, winded and sucking air, heads drooping, and started walking back to their previously-grazed picket place. Tatum stood with the Hawken cradled across his chest and watched the two young Indians scamper up the steep bank of the arroyo and make their escape. He chuckled at them and turned to pack up for the night's journey. He knew the young men would probably remain silent about their failed attempt at horse stealing and even if they told, he would be long gone by the time they could make it back.

This night's journey started a bit earlier than most, what with full daylight showing as the sun blazed its last rays in long shafts of brilliance that stretched through the clouds that caught and held the last colors of the day. The prairie was painted with colors seldom seen on a normal day's travel and Tatum enjoyed the display of God's majesty at the end of this day. And as the sun tucked its colorful robe of light behind the horizon and the shadows reached their full length, Tatum marked his next landmark in his mind and let the horses stretch their legs for the night's travel. As darkness settled over the flats, the quietness of the night was a welcome blanket of peace. One by one the sounds of nocturnal animals welcomed Tatum with their harmony of nature. He smiled at the yips of the coyote followed by its lonesome wail and he waited for an answer and was startled when it came from nearby. His sorrel did a quick side-step of surprise but never missed a stride. A nearby bluff, silhouetted in the moonlight, yielded a cloud of bats coming from their dark lair deep within the folds of the bluff and taking flight to their chosen location for the night's feast. They fluttered overhead and disappeared into the shadows of the distant cottonwoods that rode the bank of a nearby creek.

As Tatum topped a slight rise, he spotted a light in the distance that he readily identified as a campfire and then there were others, a total of five in all. Whoever was camped there was getting an early start on their day's travel and Tatum knew he had to find good cover just in case they were coming his way. Within a short distance he came to a sizeable stream with cottonwoods, willows and alders along the bank and thick enough clusters to provide good cover and shelter for the rest of the night and the following daylight hours. He found a suitable campsite, picketed the animals and turned in, choosing to forego his usual breakfast and need of a fire. He reminded himself to sleep light, just in case.

CHAPTER TEN
TRADERS

IT WAS A LITTLE PAST MIDNIGHT WHEN HE SPOTTED THE remains of their fires; just like the night before there were five campfires that had burnt down to smoldering coals. But as the clouds hid the big moon, the coals glowed and gave away the campsite. Tatum dismounted and ground-tied his horses to slip to the top of the rise and get a better look. He lay on his belly and surveyed the camp, counting twelve big freighter wagons, more than thirty occupied bedrolls, and at least two men on guard. Rastus had told him about the Sante Fe Trail and he had followed it since he came to the Arkansas River. These were apparently traders making their way to Sante Fe with a considerable load of trade goods. He watched for a moment longer, taking in the sight and considering the group of traders. Crabbing back away from the crest of the hill and rising to retrieve his horses, he decided to swing wide of their camp and continue to follow the trail. But because of his aversion for being around too many people, he determined to stay well away from the trail but near enough to easily make his way and follow the proven path.

The bluff rose to his left and the pillars of stone cast long shadows in the moonlight and the timbered draw beckoned to Tatum in answer to his search for a campsite. He had left the freighters well behind and enjoyed the peaceful night's journey. Now, he spotted a thin game trail that led into the dark maw of the small canyon and followed it as it rose on a stair-step path toward the top of the bluff. Just below the rimrock that was the source of the strewn boulders below, a flat shoulder covered with buffalo grass offered a place of rest. He heard the trickle of a spring as the water tumbled into a small pool and he stepped down. He arched his back and stretched his tired limbs, then de-rigged the horses and tethered them within reach of the water. Too tired to fix any breakfast, he grasped a handful of jerky from his pack and began to munch as he rolled out his blankets. He looked around and, satisfied with the site, he reclined on the bedroll, pulled his hat over his eyes and bid good-night to the creatures of the night that had been his traveling companions.

The sudden rattle of gunfire brought him fully awake, unconsciously reaching for his Hawken as he sat up. He looked around in the full daylight of mid-morning, saw his horses with heads up and ears pricked forward but, seeing nothing nearby and knowing the sound was farther away, he looked to the top of the bluff and started up the trail. With his possibles bag and powder horn in hand, he moved stealthily upward to the flat top of the small mesa. He draped the bag and horn over his head and across his chest and in a crouch made his way to the edge. He dropped to his hands and knees and crawled to peer over the rimrock to the scene below.

The caravan of freighters had been stopped by a passing herd of buffalo and now the outriders and some aboard the freighters were shooting indiscriminately into the herd, their frustration at being stopped taken out by killing the many animals in their way. The roar of gunfire accomplished the intended purpose of the freighters and the herd lifted as one massive brown blanket that covered the prairie and began to rumble in a stampede away from the killers. Some of the outriders gave chase and shot more of the wooly beasts as they sought to escape. The cloud of dust from the stampeding buffalo rose over the scene of the slaughter as if attempting to hide the senseless carnage perpetrated by the traders.

Tatum shook his head at the absurdity of the act before him, thinking of the stupidity of the white men that allowed their impatience to overtake reason and let their blood lust control them. As he considered what he had witnessed, he started to rise, but something caught his attention back in the timber at the edge of the bluff. There was another ravine hidden from the view of the flats, holding some juniper and pinion and a sizeable group of mounted Indians. There were three of them lying on the ridge along the edge of the ravine and watching the actions of the traders and muleskinners. Tatum quickly counted just less than twenty warriors and knew they held their place because of the numbers of traders and their weapons. They watched the outriders return and shout at the muleskinners and as two of the riders stepped down beside one of the downed buffalo, they motioned the freighters to keep moving.

The big freight wagons, each pulled by a six-up of mules, negotiated their way around and through the scattered carcasses to resume their trek toward Sante Fe. The two outriders quickly butchered the buffalo, stripping the carcass of the best cuts of meat and, using part of the hide, made bundles to carry behind their saddles. Tatum noticed another pair of outriders butchering a second buffalo in much the same way and before long the four men were on their way to catch up with the freight caravan, leaving behind at least a dozen untouched carcasses of buffalo.

The Indians waited until the wagons were out of sight, then came from the ravine and rode toward the downed buffalo. Tatum had witnessed two of the warriors ride off in a southerly direction but the rest went to the scene of the slaughter and began the work of butchering the other carcasses. He continued to watch, learning how they so skillfully worked on the buffalo. He was surprised to see them almost totally skin the animal by splitting the skin from neck to tail and peeling it back by attaching a rawhide rope to the edges of the hide that were on the legs, then using a horse to pull the hide back as they slipped their knives between the hide and the meat. Then rolling the animal over, again with the aid of the horse, they finished the skinning. Only then did they open the chest and stomach to retrieve the usable organs and intestines. Before the men had completed the first buffalo, another large group of Indians that included women and children, joined in the work of butchering the many carcasses.

It was easy to tell by their actions and animated conversation they were angry with the white men that did the killing, but they were also thankful that the buffalo would be a welcome addition to their larder. Seeing nothing new and believing he was safe where he was, Tatum decided to try to resume his sleeping before nightfall came and he was on the trail again. He slid back away from the edge and walked down the trail to his campsite, surveyed the area and saw his horses unalarmed and cropping grass, and turned back to his blankets.

When he awoke, he knew something had disturbed him and he did not move. He could see his horses and they were heads up and ears forward looking at something but they were not afraid, just curious. Under his blankets he gripped the Paterson Colt and slowly rolled to his back for a better view of the clearing. There were at least five Indians standing in a semi-circle at the edge of the clearing and watching him as he moved. Two had nocked arrows and partially drawn bows, ready for any sudden move. As he sat up, he kept the Colt under the blanket and spoke, "Howdy, fellas. What brings you to my camp?"

No one moved or answered his question. As he moved to stand, still holding his blanketed pistol before him, he noticed two more standing near his horses. He remembered Rastus' teaching about leaving things around to warn of intruders and he had scattered some pine cones and twigs, but these Indians had avoided them and moved silently into his camp. *They musta' followed my trail up from the bottom. Gonna have to remember that and cover my trail next time, if there is a next time,* he thought. One of the men before him spoke, "Why you here?" Tatum was surprised at the man's use of English and noted his appearance. All the men had their hair cut away from the sides of their heads and over their ears, giving the appearance of baldness. But the tops had some locks standing tall and others had braids going down the back; several had feathers or other decorations in their hair. Some had breast plates of small bones and others had decorated bands around their necks. All had at least a long vest of decorated and fringed leather that hung below their waists, and their leggings had an overhanging breechcloth. Most of the moccasins had beaded patterns and they held a variety of weapons. The speaker had a Kentucky-style rifle but others had lances or war clubs or bows and arrows. Most had tomahawks and knives in their waistbands and all of them scowled at the white man before them.

Tatum answered the query, "Why, I'm just passing through on my way to the mountains," and motioned to the west and the mountains beyond.

"You come with us," directed the speaker and motioned for him to get his packs and his horses. Tatum complied, sticking the Colt into his waistband as he turned toward the horses. He saddled the packhorse and then the sorrel and, with reins and lead-rope in hand, followed the Indians back down the trail he used to ascend the bluff. With three before him and four behind, Tatum knew he would accomplish nothing by trying to flee and decided to bide his time and see what he could learn of these Indians. He was curious as to what tribe they were and about their customs and ways. *Maybe I can learn a bit about 'em, if they don't kill me, that is,* he thought as he followed the men toward the scene of the slaughter.

CHAPTER ELEVEN
KIOWA

THE KIOWA VILLAGE WAS ABOUT THREE MILES SOUTH OF THE bluff and lay in a wide valley surrounded by thick growth of juniper, pinion, and cedar. The nearby hills provided good cover and the village was well concealed. Tatum stared at the many tepees with a variety of painted patterns making each lodge unique but they were the same with the flapped openings all facing to the east and the top flaps directing the smoke from the fires within. Tatum and his horses were in the middle of the long line of horses and riders returning to the village with the bounty from the buffalo kill. Many of the animals, led by women, pulled travois loaded with fresh meat and hides. Those remaining in the village cheered those returning with the buffalo, knowing the bounty would be cause for a feast of celebration. Two warriors rode beside Tatum and directed him to stop near a lodge that appeared empty. While the others had lances with shields near the entry—willow backrests near cook fires and other accouterments that told of the occupants—this one, though decorated, had nothing nearby.

As Tatum stepped down, he was goaded toward the entry

and the motions of the men told him to enter. They had taken the reins and lead rope for his horses from him and pushed him into the entry. He stumbled through the opening and stopped as he entered. He stood and looked around at a bare lodge with a fire ring in the middle and one palette of blankets on the far side and nothing else to indicate this was anything but a place for captives. He turned and stuck his head out of the entry and saw a warrior standing at the side who motioned him back inside. All he could do was walk to the blankets and be seated and wait to see what would happen next.

His wait wasn't as long as expected when three warriors stepped through the entry and stood before him. He slowly stood to face them and noticed one of the men held his longbow at his side. It had the bowstring wound around the upper limb as he had secured it for traveling. The man that spoke was the same as the leader of the hunters that had originally confronted Tatum and he now looked at the young man before him and asked, "What is this?" and motioned toward the bow.

Tatum smiled and said, "Let me show you," lifting his hand toward the bow but the man holding it pulled back away from him. Tatum continued and said, "It is called a longbow. I use it for hunting."

The speaker turned to the man on his left, obviously an elder and leader of the people, and said, "Doh‰san, . . ." and was waved silent by the man. Tatum looked at the elder and asked, "Is that your name, Doh‰san? My name is Tatum," and held out his hand to shake in greeting but was ignored by the leader.

The elder spoke in their own language to the younger man that had addressed Tatum in English and also with hand motions instructing him to have Tatum follow them and show how to use the bow. Tatum understood and followed the men from the lodge and stopped at they stood before him and handed him the longbow. He looked at them and removed the string from the upper limb of the bow attached to the lower bow nock and, putting the end of the bow to the right side of his right foot, he stepped through the bow; using his leg and upper arm strength, he bent the bow to attach the string to the bow stave. He stepped back through the bow and handed it back to the warrior that previously held it. Tatum watched, grinning, as the warrior tried to pull the bow string back and was surprised at the tautness of the string and his difficulty trying to draw the bow. The others looked at him and the speaker who had been addressed as Settan reached for the bow and also tried to draw the bow. All the men, and others that had gathered around, looked at Tatum questioningly. He grinned and asked the speaker, "Could you set up a target of some sort and I'll demonstrate?"

Settan turned to one of the bystanders and addressed him in their language to set up a target but Tatum motioned him to set up two and Settan nodded to the man to set up two targets. Tatum asked, "Can I have my quiver?"

Settan looked at the young man and motioned to another to fetch the quiver and the man turned quickly and ran to a nearby lodge to retrieve the quiver of arrows. Tatum noted the lodge where his stuff had been stashed and waited for the young man to return with the arrows. He looked to the other man that was setting up the targets and said to Settan, "Have him take one about thirty paces farther." Settan hollered out to the target setter to do as bidden and turned back to the white man. Tatum looked at him and said, "Now, have one of your warriors with a bow and arrow shoot with me. I'll take the far target and he can take the near one." Again, Settan instructed a nearby warrior to come alongside with his bow and arrow.

Tatum instructed, "We," and motioned to himself and the

other bowman, "will shoot at the same time on your signal."
He nocked an arrow and lifted his bow as did the man beside
him but while the Indian held his left arm extended and
pulled the bowstring back almost to his ear, Tatum anchored
his right arm with the bowstring and stepped into his bow by
pushing the bow forward to give a full draw. Settan instantly
shouted his signal and both men released their arrows.

A collective gasp rose from the bystanders as they saw
Tatum's arrow and the other arrow strike their targets simul-
taneously and Tatum's arrow went completely through the
bull-hide target while the Indian's arrow penetrated to the
fletching. Tatum lowered his bow alongside his hip and
smiled his satisfaction at the surprise of the gathered crowd.
They muttered their amazement and wonder at the white
man's expertise with the longbow and the power of the
unusual weapon. Tatum looked at Settan and asked, "Could
you have your man retrieve my arrow and move the target
another thirty paces?"

When the crowd saw the target being moved, they looked
at the white man and the target and began talking among
themselves. Several were nodding their heads in disbelief
and motioning with their hands about the unusual moves of
the young man. When the target was ready, Tatum nodded at
the other archer and indicated for him to take a shot at the
far target. He complied, but lifted his bow to give a high arch
to the arrow, released the arrow and watched it climb the
arch and drop short of the target. Tatum nocked another
arrow, repeated his moves and let fly with the arrow whis-
pering its way in a straight line to the target and again
piercing it through. The crowd muttered their oohs and aahs
at the amazing display of the young man.

The circle of men looked at one another and at the white
man and at a nod from Doh‰san, Settan said to Tatum,
"Long Bow, you will come feast with us. We would learn

more of this bow you use." Tatum grinned at Settan's use of the description of his longbow as his name, but nodded his head to follow. He quickly unstrung the bow with the same movements used to string it, wrapped the bowstring around the upper limb and followed the men to a central circle of the village.

As they feasted, Tatum shared all he knew about making a longbow, stressing the type of wood, how the outer sapwood provides the tension and the rounded heartwood resists compression and provides greater strength. He hoped they understood, but at least he could tell they were appreciative of his sharing his knowledge. During their discussions, he learned that Settan was Little Bear in English, and Doh‰san meant Little Mountain. These were the Ka'igwu people, or Kiowa, and this band were the ThÛq‡hyÚp, or Men of the Cold. Settan was a part of the Ton-Kon-Gah or Black Leg warrior society. Although it would be much to remember, he was pleased they were willing to share this information with him.

As the feast concluded, Tatum, or Long Bow as he was now known, asked to leave explaining to his new friends that he preferred to travel at night. They were surprised at his revelation, but dispatched some men to get his horses and gear so he could depart. As he mounted to leave, Little Mountain noticed his tomahawk and the beadwork and asked to see it. Tatum handed it to the chief and watched as he examined the weapon. Little Mountain looked at Tatum and with sign language, interpreted by Little Bear, asked where the tomahawk was from and was surprised to find it was a gift from the Osage. Tatum didn't know, but the eagle symbol on the handle spoke of the high rank of the gift-giver and Little Mountain was impressed. He motioned to a woman standing nearby and she trotted off to return holding something behind her back. She passed it to Doh‰san who lifted it to Tatum and he spoke, "For Long Bow, to remember the Ka'igwu." It was a buffalo hide war shield with the design of a charging buffalo painted in bright colors. Tufts of hair adorned the circular edge and Tatum was sure they were scalp locks. He looked at the chief and said, "I am honored, and Long Bow will never forget the great Ka'igwu and especially the great chief Doh‰san."

The chief and others stepped back and lifted their arms, open palms forward to indicate he was to go in peace. Tatum gave the same sign, reined his mount around, and trotted away from the village. Dusk was settling across the land as Tatum looked over his shoulder at the village now well behind him, turned back to the trail before him and took a deep, shoulder lifting breath and said, "Thanks, Lord, for giving me new friends."

It was another clear moonlit night and the trail easy to follow as Tatum again listened for his distant companions of the coyotes, owls, cicadas and others. This was his time and his place and he enjoyed the coolness of the evening but looked forward to new country and the distant mountains. Life was good and he was greatly enjoying himself, but he often thought of his father and how he would have enjoyed this trip and the wonderful country. *Guess I'll just have to live it for the both of us,* he thought as he looked at the stars searching for his guiding light.

CHAPTER TWELVE
BENT'S FORT

IT HAD BEEN A MOSTLY UNEVENTFUL WEEK SINCE LEAVING THE village of the Kiowa except for one confrontation with a hunting party of the tribe. But when they recognized the sign of Doh‰san on the war shield that hung from the pommel of Tatum's saddle, they gave him safe passage. Had it not been for that meeting, Tatum would have called the past week almost monotonous. Yet travel in the frontier always held interest for a student of the wild, and Tatum considered himself a student of the wilderness in every sense. Each day seemed to give new discoveries; whether animals or plants or vistas, Tatum never lost interest in his frontier education.

He stayed south of the Arkansas River but within sight of the roadway known at the Sante Fe Trail. With several feeder creeks coming from the southern bluffs and the far mountains, he seldom had to go to the Arkansas for water, and usually found suitable campsites among the bluffs and dark green timber of the plains. On his usual early morning hunt in the dim light of pre-dawn, he bagged a couple of the long-eared jackrabbits that always made Tatum chuckle at their big feet and long ears. As he stood atop a rise to survey the surrounding country, he spotted what he believed was Bent's Fort. Since his brief visit with the old trapper Rastus, Bent's Fort had been his long sought for goal of his journey. Rastus had said, "Bent's Fort'll be yore jumpin' off place, boy. From there, you can see the mountains an' find yore way to them beeeutiful Rockies, yessir." Tatum shaded his eyes and looked in the distance and as the day began to show its new sunlit face, far in the distance rose two mountains, unmistakable in their grandeur with the granite tips reaching toward the blue-grey of the morning sky. As he looked, the rising sun seemed to paint the tips with dusty pink to add to the beauty. He let his gaze wander along the jagged horizon and he saw another tall mountain stretching toward the growing blue canopy. He sucked in a deep breath and let the smile spread across his face showing the wonder of the youth. He felt himself grow as he stood tall with his pride of accomplishment for there, just beyond his reach, were the Rocky Mountains. He thought of his father and knew if he was standing by his side, he too would swell with pride.

Tatum turned and trotted back to his campsite to build a fire and broil his morning's meal and brew a pot of coffee. As he thought about the mountains and the days behind him, he wondered if he would be able to go to sleep this day. *Maybe I'll have to go on to the fort and re-supply, then find a camp. Yeah, that's what I'll do; then I'll be ready to head for the mountains,* thought Tatum. The mountains seemed so near yet he knew distances could be difficult to determine, but he wasn't on a schedule anyway. He would savor every day of his trip even more since the mountains were now within sight.

His eagerness got the better of him and he was soon on his way to the fort. This would be his first time to be with white men since he started his journey except for his brief time with Rastus. But he knew this would be different, hopefully. He crossed the Purgatoire River, turned north and when the fort was well in sight, crossed the Arkansas River with the water no deeper than the belly of his horses. As he neared the post, he saw a cluster of tepees on the far side of the tall walls of the fort. He reined up to look at the sight before him. The massive fort was larger than he imagined and the fifteen-foot-high adobe walls with the bastion on the corner with several cannons protruding over the ledges were imposing at the least. He had never seen a structure this big and impressive. He stood in his stirrups and leaned from one side to the other to take in as much of this amazing sight as he could. There were people all around; some were Indians, both men and women, and he saw several Indian children playing some game with a hoop as they ran among the tepees. Other men, clad in buckskins and all carrying a rifle, were walking among the tepees and in and out of the open gate. He gigged his mount forward and walked his horses into the gate, craning his neck to look above him at the tall walls and marveled at the massive gates and the four-foot-thick structure.

As he scanned the interior of the fort, he saw the post supported overhangs that provided a walkway around the fort walls, but also made a porch-like overhang for the various rooms that lined the interior of the walls. A simple sign that read "Trader" indicated the entry into the store and trader's post where supplies could be found. Tatum paid little attention to those within the fort, though he had attracted some attention. His hairless face betrayed his youth and although it was not unusual for young men to strike out on their own, with so many bearded and bushy mountain men and trappers, Tatum was an uncommon sight.

He tethered his horses to the hitch rail beside others and walked to the doorway, making his way inside the darkened interior. The main light came from the windows beside the door but with the back wall being the same as the fort wall, two lanterns hung on support posts to give light to the trader's counter and the conducting of his business. Two tables sat against the side wall with one occupied by two buckskin-clad mountain men while the other had a single man, quite large and inebriated, clad in a homespun shirt, canvas britches with galluses, and hobnail boots. The drunk banged his mug on the table, insisting on a refill. He was ignored by everyone, the clerk included.

While the trader was busy with another man at the counter, Tatum stood back and looked at the assortment of wares on the shelves behind the counter and along one side wall. Other goods and barrels were stacked in the corners and in front of the shelves. The clerk chewed on a smoldering pipe while the smoke seemed to circle his partially bald head as he examined some pelts for trade. When he finished he spoke softly to the trapper, apparently giving a price, which brought a nod from him and the trader stacked some coins on the counter which were quickly scooped up by the trapper.

The clerk looked at the young man and said, "Well, youngster, what can I do ye fer?"

Tatum started to speak but was interrupted by the rowdy drunk insisting on some more rum. When the clerk said, "No more for you, Smitty," and turned back to Tatum, the drunk staggered to his feet and stumbled to the counter, pushing Tatum back with, "Outta my way sonny! This is man's bizness!" and reached out for the trader who avoided his grab with a step back. As the big man dropped his elbow to the counter, he winced at the pain, and flung both arms back, hitting Tatum on the shoulder and making him stumble back a step. The big man looked at him and said, "I tol' you ta git outta my way!" as he turned to Tatum, raising his fist. Tatum didn't move or backpedal but slowly lifted his hand to the butt of his Paterson that was obscured by the tail of his jacket.

"Leave him alone," ordered the clerk.

"I'm gonna teach you a lesson, you young whippersnapper!" snarled the drunk and started toward Tatum. He reached out and grabbed Tatum's jacket collar and cocked his free arm, readying to strike a blow to the young man's face, but was stopped when he heard another voice from behind him that said, "Smitty, if you hit that young man, you might not live long enough to regret it!" Without letting go of Tatum's collar, he turned to face the new threat and looked at one of the men sitting at the table, clutching a metal mug and grinning at the big drunk.

"You stay outta this, Carson!" barked the drunk and saw the man lean back and lift both hands as he said, "Then don't say I didn't warn you," and nodded his head in the direction of the fracas. As the big man turned back to Tatum, he heard a metallic click that made him drop his gaze to see the Colt, hammer cocked and barrel now pressed against his midriff. He looked back at the cold eyes of the young man and began to stutter, "Uh, uh, now hold on there, boy," as he uncurled his fingers that held Tatum's collar. "You don't need to be usin' that. I weren't gonna do nuthin, honest," pleaded the drunk as he backed away from the counter. He looked at the men at the table, at the man behind the counter, all of whom were grinning at the man's predicament, and staggered to the door to leave.

Tatum replaced the Colt in his waistband and looking at the clerk, started with his list of goods. He knew this would be the only supply point for his journey into the mountains and he focused on what he deemed most important as he was nearing the last of the money his father had set aside. After the clerk filled his order, the tally left Tatum with little money, but he was well supplied. As he started to leave, the man at the table who had spoken up for him waved him over and said, "How 'bout joinin' us for a drink, young man?"

"Thank you, sir, but I don't drink. Thank you just the same," and started to turn away.

"How 'bout some coffee then; you drink coffee don't you?" asked the light-haired man with blue eyes.

"Yessir, I do. I'd be proud to join you," replied Tatum as he seated himself at the table. He was impressed with the friendliness of the man who smiled and spoke softly as he waved to the clerk to bring some coffee.

"And what brings you to this country? Trappin', explorin', or just out for a walk? Oh, and by the way, they call me Carson, Kit Carson, and this is the fella what built this here fort, William Bent."

Tatum extended his hand as he said, "I'm Tatum Saint, from Missouri. And to answer your question, I'm just goin' to the mountains to get away from people."

Carson laughed at the young man's explanation and said, "You know, I weren't much older'n you when I came out. Joined a caravan of traders on the Sante Fe Trail an' ended up here with this rascal," referring to Bent that sat beside him. "I reckon your reason is better'n most. Too many younkers come out lookin' ta' make their fortune and end up feedin' the bears. You know anything about livin' in the mountains, Tatum?"

"Well, not so much as far as the mountains go, but a little about livin' alone in the wilderness."

"Didju come all this way by yourself?"

"Yessir."

"Any trouble with Injuns?" asked Carson, looking a bit sideways at the young man, judging his honesty.

"No trouble, really. Visited with the Osage and the Kiowa, but no trouble really."

"Visited? Folks don't just visit the Osage and the Kiowa.

Why them's two o' the baddest bunch o' Injuns to run up against!" he responded as he leaned on the table looking at Tatum.

"If you say so, but I made friends with 'em easier I did any white man, like you just saw," nodding his head toward the counter.

Carson looked at Bent and nodded his head as he asked his friend, "You ever hear such a story as that?"

While the two men looked at one another, Tatum pulled the tomahawk from his belt, laid it on the table, and said, "This was a gift from Black Buffalo of the Osage, and I have a war shield on my saddle that Doh‰ san, of the Kiowa, gave me."

Carson looked at him unbelieving and said, "Doh‰ san? You mean Little Mountain?"

"That's right, Little Mountain."

Carson looked down at the tomahawk and picked it up to examine and the two men looked it over and looked at one another as they marveled at the tomahawk and its crafts-manship. Carson said, "It sure looks like something the Osage would do," and looked at Tatum and said, "And you have a war shield from the Kiowa?"

Tatum rose from his seat and went to retrieve the war shield and brought it to the two skeptical men. Before he held it, Carson saw the shield and looked at the young man with wonder. As Tatum passed it to him, Carson took the shield and held it almost reverently as he examined the shield and the scalp-locks. He looked up at Tatum, now standing beside the table, and said, "And Little Mountain gave this to you?"

Tatum simply nodded his head as he watched the two men of the wilderness shake their heads in amazement. Carson said, "Son, you've done what no other white man has ever done before. That's sumpin' that is," nodding toward the shield.

The remainder of the morning was spent getting acquainted with Carson and Bent and learning about the ways of the trader and the country. As time approached for the noon meal, Bent invited Carson and Tatum to join him for the meal in his quarters, and the men gratefully accepted. After the meal, Tatum excused himself by explaining his habit of traveling at night, and left to retrieve his horses and supplies. Carson followed him to the trader's and suggested they join up on the morrow for a hunt, and they agreed to meet at dawn by the front gate.

THE TWO MEN WERE BELLY DOWN ON THE SLIGHT KNOLL AND eyeing a small herd of antelope. Tatum told Kit about his first experience with the goat of the plains and Kit chuckled, "Ya' see, Tate, them goats yonder have eyesight a whole lot better'n yours or mine. Some say they can see like you would with a spyglass, an' they're fast! Faster'n any horse you'll ever find, but they's curious too, an' that's how you kin git 'em. Now, you just crawl up thar," and pointed to the flat of the crest of the hill, "tie this here neckerchief on the end o' yer muzzle and sit real still, an' I mean still. Cuz if'n you move the least bit, you'll lose 'em, but they'll see that rag wavin' in the breeze an' they'll come to check it out an' when they gits close 'nuff, you can shoot 'em."

Tatum looked at his new friend, searching his eyes for some indication he was kidding but, finally believing Kit was serious, Tatum did as he was instructed. Once seated, he remained motionless and watched the distant herd. He sat for close to half an hour and was surprised to see the antelope slowly making their way nearer and nearer. Finally, he heard a whisper, "Just a little closer, an' you can take yore shot. Butcha gotta be quick about it, wait for the lead buck thar to look away, then do it." The buck would take a couple of steps, stand immobile and watching, then would drop his head to snatch a bite of buffalo grass and casually take a couple of steps in a slightly different direction but closer, and stop again. When he dropped his head, Tatum brought the Hawken down, aimed and fired just as the buck leaned away to flee, but the bullet soared true and dropped the hapless buck before he could complete his escape. The rest of the herd disappeared in a moment leaving only a rising puff of dust to tell of their flight.

"See thar, Tate, toldja!" declared Carson as he stood behind the still seated Tatum. The young man looked at Carson and replied, "I would never have thought that would work, but it sure did." The men started walking to the carcass and Carson began to point out distant landmarks. "Now, lookee yonder, there at them two mountains, them's the Spanish Peaks. Now, just to the south of 'em, is where the Purgatoire River starts and that's mighty purty country round behind them peaks." He pointed north of the peaks and continued, "Now that cut in the mountains just north o' them Spanish Peaks is where the Huerfano and Cucharas Rivers come from and there's a good pass o'er the Sangre de Cristo mountains, that's them what runs down towards Taos and past, an' up north to the rest o' the Rockies. And that pass takes you into the San Luis valley, and the old Spanish trail leads on west o' there."

Tatum looked at Carson and asked, "Sangre de Cristo? What's that mean?"

Carson grinned at the young man's ignorance but willingness to learn and explained, "Them mountains was named by a black robe priest when the Injuns was 'bout to kill him.

He looked at the mountains just as the sun was droppin' in the west an' the colors of the sunset showed on the snow-capped mountains and made 'em look kinda red. The priest thought it was the blood of Christ an' said so, and after that even the Injuns called 'em Sangre de Cristo, or Blood of Christ.

"Now, let's get the butcherin' o' that goat done, an' mebbe we can find us some buffler."

The men continued their hunt and Carson willingly answered all the questions of the young man he began to think of as his apprentice. Tatum quizzed the experienced mountain man about hunting, animals, wilderness and winter; when the subject of winter was broached, Carson began to expand his comments considerably. "'Bout the only thing good 'bout winters in the mountains is the grizzlies are hid away n' sleepin'; other'n that, winter in the mountains can be a killer." Carson continued his wilderness instruction with a few tall timber tales that illustrated the dangers of the mountains. "Ya' see, that snow gits so deep up high, an' the wind blows o'er the top and makes these ridges, and if there's anythin' that disturbs them ridges, like a loud noise or sumpin', they just break off an' come slidin' down and bringin' ever'thin' with it, trees, rocks, more snow, everthin'. It's called a avalanche and it destroys ever'thin' in its path. Why, I seen 'em bury a whole herd of elk onct, an' them elk was froze up till spring. But when the green-up started, they thawed out and ran off just like nothin' happened." He cackled at his funny and looked at his hunting partner. Tatum just grinned and added, "I guess that's what you call puttin' up meat for the winter." Carson cackled and broke into a belly laugh that was contagious and both men enjoyed the moment.

"But all kiddin' aside, Tate, muh boy, 'fore winter comes,

you need to have yoreself a warm place, lot's o' firewood, an' plenty o' meat. And don't forget your animals there, they need shelter n' food too. In the winter time if ya ain't got nuthin' else, horses'll eat the inner thin bark from cotton-woods, or you can singe off the spikes from prickly pear cactus, or you gotta dig under the snow fer grass, but they gotta eat too. When th' Quakies turn gold, that's yore warnin', but when they shed their leaves, it's a comin'. Now you, you can eat just 'bout anythin' that walks or crawls or hops or swims, but horses now, they're a mite more particlar'.

"Now, when it comes to Injuns, you've been purty lucky. But now you're headin' into country that's got some mean 'uns. There's Comanche," and he motioned to the south end of the Sangre de Cristo, "and over yonder cross that pass is the valley of the San Luis. The south end of that is Jicarilla Apache, and the west end of it has the Weeminuche and the Mouache Ute. Now, hereabouts, the fort there does a lot o' tradin' with the Arapaho and the Cheyenne, but them moun-tains have lots of Injuns cuz ever' tribe travels to other tribes' territory and raids the villages takin' horses and captives, women 'specially."

Tatum felt he was getting the education of a lifetime just by spending time with the experienced Kit Carson. He didn't know that Carson was already building himself quite a repu-tation and his explorations would take him all the way to the Pacific Ocean and back again. But, for now, it was enough that this well-experienced man was willing to share his knowledge with a young but eager student.

At Carson's suggestion, Tatum demonstrated his skill with the bow by bagging a wild turkey at about eighty yards and the teacher was well impressed with the expertise of the student. By mid-day they had one antelope, one turkey, one mule deer, and one buffalo. Carson had brought two pack-horses and they were well loaded for his return. Tatum had bundled a generous cut of buffalo and a haunch of antelope for his immediate needs and to smoke for the days to come. When the time came that they were to part, Carson said to his protégé, "Tate, I think you've got it in you to do well in the mountains. Always be careful, and watch your backtrail and mind what I've tried to tell you."

"I'm mighty thankful, Kit. You've taught me a lot in such a short time, and I hope we'll see each other sometime soon," and he reached out his hand to shake, adding, "Thanks again."

"You're welcome, Tate, an' like we say in the mountains, keep yore topknot on!"

Carson put his heels to his horse and leading his packhorses in a string, headed back to the fort. Tatum watched him for a short way, then turned toward the mountains, following the directions of his new friend toward the Spanish Peaks that beckoned in the distance. He knew it would be three or four days before he would be there, but his excitement drove him on, knowing he was fulfilling a long-held dream of both his and his father's.

With the vista of the mountains before him, he had decided to start traveling in the daylight hours. With the moon waning to its last quarter, traveling at night was more difficult and after seeing some of the prairie dog villages with the many holes that could break a horse's leg, he thought the safest bet would be to travel during the day. But for now, he needed a campsite and the trees above the arroyo and along the rising hillside showed promise. After stopping and picketing his horses, he started a small fire for some fresh broiled buffalo steak and some refreshing java. While waiting on the steaks, he fashioned a drying rack and began slicing the remaining buffalo and antelope into the thin strips necessary for smoking. Carson had pointed out some mesquite bushes and said, "You won't find those very often this far north, but they grow a lot down toward Mexico.

That's mesquite and awfully good for smokin' yore meat. You might try it with that buffler." He started a small fire near a cluster of juniper that would dissipate the smoke and as the coals glowed, he placed the rack over the coals, hung the strips of meat and laid the mesquite on the coals. Now it was time for supper.

CHAPTER FOURTEEN
WAGONS

THE TERRAIN BEFORE HIM WAS DRY AND DUSTY, A FAR CRY from the green forested hills of the Ozarks in Missouri. Where there were the thick green woods and grassy meadows with everything showing shades of green, here there was dry flatlands that held rocks, cactus, and dust. Every step of the horses lifted individual clouds of grey dust that gathered together to mark his passing for anyone and anything within several miles to see. Having become accustomed to passing through the land as inconspicuously as possible and mostly completely unseen, now he seemed to be announcing his presence.

A dust devil danced across the flats and followed the contours of a dry arroyo, picking up tumbleweeds and dropping them indiscriminately. Tatum watched, thinking it a miniature version of a tornado seen in his youth. As the sorrel shuffled along with his rolling gait, Tatum scanned the flats in every direction seeing nothing but the same thing that lay around him. He noted the variety of cacti, cholla, prickly pear, hedgehog, small barrel, and more of the same. Overhead he spotted some turkey buzzards floating on the updraft from the hot flats and looking for a meal. Before him he saw a jackrabbit scamper from a clump of rabbit brush with a coyote in pursuit, and they both disappeared over the lip of the twisting dry arroyo. This was a wild land but one that held its own beauty and mystique.

It was near the end of the third day after leaving Bent's Fort that Tatum entered the pine forest that blanketed the flanks of the Spanish Peaks. At last he was in the mountains, and he stood in his stirrups to look up the rising talus slope above. It stuck out from the trees like a sentinel of the plains and Tatum determined to circle below it until he found a way to the top. Once there, he ground tied the horses, walked to the promontory and looked over the vast flatlands in the east to the mountains in the north and the forested slope below him and to the west of the mountain. He sucked in the cool mountain air and stood with hands on hips and surveyed the panorama like a king surveying his domain. He smiled at the thought and wanted to shout to the heavens that he had arrived.

Something caught his eye in the distance and he watched as what appeared to be a long white snake slowly moving toward the mountains. He went back to his horse and retrieved his spyglass from the saddle bags and returned to the promontory. He dropped to one knee, rested his elbow on the knee to stabilize the spyglass and looked in the distance. A wagon train of more than twenty wagons was winding its way toward the pass between Tatum and the Sangre de Cristo mountains that marched northward. He watched as the wagonmaster signaled those behind him to circle up for the night's camp. They were on a flat that was fed by a small stream and the wagons were moved into a circle near the stream and nearby cover of trees. Tatum seated himself and continued to watch through his spyglass as the many folks of the train busied themselves, unharnessing the mules and horses, taking them to water and others fetching firewood for campfires. He couldn't make out the appearance of the many people, just that several were women with long dresses and some were children. *Looks like several families, probably the wagon train that Carson said left the fort a couple days ago. They must be makin' for the old Spanish trail that Carson talked about. He said that led west to California; guess them folks are lookin' to make a new home way out yonder. That's gonna be quite a trip,* thought Tatum.

Looking below and behind his promontory, Tatum decided to descend the mountain to the valley just west of the peaks, thinking that would be the headwaters of the Cucharas River that Carson had spoken of and would be a good campsite. He looked at the position of the sun, calculated he still had three to four hours of daylight and mounted up to move off the mountain. As he started down the mountainside, following a game trail through the pines, he thought about the wagon train and wondered why they made camp so early in the day with so much time left to travel. *Maybe they got some kinda trouble or sumpin'. Oh well, none of my affair.*

Just as Carson said, the valley behind the Spanish Peaks was lush and fertile, truly a beautiful place and with an abundance of game. As Tatum rode into the open meadow on the trail leading from the black timber, he immediately reined up and stared in disbelief. There before him was a herd of the royalty of the mountains, wapiti or elk. A massive bull with antlers that stretched back more than the length of his body and with tall tines that stood like a rank of guards and pointed heavenward warned of the weapons that he would wield as the guardian of his harem. The dark brown cape that draped over his neck and down his chest added to the impressive stance of the animal that was every bit as tall and muscular as the very horse Tatum rode; the tapered torso that stretched to the rear haunches that bespoke strength and speed ended with the yellowish white camouflage of his rump. He was a majestic figure and he watched the herd before him that had younger bulls, cows and yearling calves, all grazing without concern and enjoying the waning light of the day.

Tatum stood in his stirrups as he looked over the herd, taking in the amazing view of such impressive animals. The herd numbered well over a hundred, far too many to count and no need of a tally. There was no fear shown, and Tatum knew they had few enemies, save the mountain lion, grizzly, and man. But the weapons wielded by the herd bull would give any predator pause and reason to look for easier game. Tatum reined his horse to follow the tree line and skirt the herd as he looked for his own campsite. The Cucharas River, a good-sized creek by Ozark standards, chuckled over the rocks as the clear water cascaded to find its way from the mountains to the plains below. Lined by willows, aspen and an occasional alder, it was an idyllic scene and Tatum easily found an opening in the creekside brush and soon made his camp.

With a sense of safety combined with hunger, Tatum opted for a better supper than usual. He dug the Dutch oven and deep pot from the pack and started his preparations. He built his fire and readied his gear and fixings. He mixed up some cornmeal dough for some biscuits and set the Dutch oven aside to await some coals. Then he put some chunks of buffalo, wild turnips, onions, and yarrow root in the pot, added water and hung it over the fire. He dragged some coals aside, sat the Dutch oven on them, and scooped other coals onto the lid and sat back to await the percolating coffee. As he sat on the log, he smiled to himself as he thought about what had transpired in the last several weeks and all the experiences and learning that occurred on the way. And now he was in the mountains, yeah!

His mind wandered to the wagon train and he wondered why they came to mind; it was as if he had some premonition about the people on the train. What if there was some kind of trouble? Of course, wherever there were people, especially white people, there would be trouble of some kind. But the reason he was here was to get away from people, not to get involved with them and their problems. But still, something was nagging at him. He didn't understand why, but maybe tomorrow he would ride over that direction and take a better look. Besides, he had spotted those four big mountains on the other side of that wide saddle that held the pass Carson spoke of and he thought they warranted a better look. Those mountains were the sentinels of the valley and seemed to stand like guards over the entrance to the wide park of the San Luis. When he gave them a brief look with the spyglass, he saw they still held snow in the upper reaches and the splashes of white against the blue grey of the granite just added to their beauty. Tatum knew he would spend much of his time just exploring the many mountains and learning to become a part of the wilderness.

He watched as his horses rolled in the grass, wiping the sweat from their backs and refreshing themselves. He looked down at his hands and the legs of his buckskins, then at the water of the stream and thought it was about time for him to get a good soaking. He couldn't even remember when he last had a dip, then he thought of the time after burying his father and realized it had been well over a month since his last bath. He chuckled to himself and thought about what his mother would have said about his failure. "Now, young man, you know, cleanliness is next to godliness!" When he asked her if that was in the Bible, she said, "Just never you mind, and make sure you get that dirt out of your ears, you have enough to grow turnips!"

His coffee was ready and he poured a cup, knowing the

rest of his supper would soon be ready and he resigned himself to taking a bath after he ate; after all, he didn't need much light to see the accumulated dirt. But that water was probably going to be mighty cold. *Oh well, the blankets will be mighty warm after that,* he surmised, and reached for his tin plate to dish up his supper.

CHAPTER FIFTEEN
VIGIL

THE CHANGE IN HIS ROUTINE FROM NIGHT TRAVEL TO DAYTIME wandering was taking some adjustment on Tatum's part and with his warm blankets feeling so good on his bare skin, he found it a bit of a challenge to roll from the warmth even though the sun had already risen. He propped himself up on his elbows, saw the horses grazing contentedly, and threw back the blankets to scamper to the willows and retrieve his buckskins that hung there to dry overnight. When he had jumped into the cold water with his bar of lye soap in the twilight of last night, he had to make quick work of scrubbing his buckskins which was contrary to Rastus' teaching and everything else. The water came from the snowmelt on the mountains and seemed to keep all its coldness all the way to his swimming hole. But he slept very well once he quit shivering and now was ready to start his day.

He wanted to spend the waning days of summer searching for what would be his winter quarters. Carson suggested finding a cave or at least a sizable overhang, and fort it up. As a last resort, he could build a cabin; he had helped his father build the work shed and he brought the tools his father used, but he liked the idea of a cave. With a cave, there was usually only one entrance to fort up and protect but with a cabin, there were four sides to be concerned with, not to mention the roof. And there was also the need for stocking up winter stores and firewood and feed for the horses, all of which would take considerable time.

He busied himself with his breakfast, warming the stew and biscuits from the night before and making fresh coffee. As he began to eat, he remembered the wagon train and his plan to take a better look at what they were doing and where they were going. Just the thought of the train brought back that uneasy feeling he couldn't quite identify, but was concerned about enough to learn more about those pilgrims.

He contemplated making his present camp a semi-permanent site and cache some of his gear and maybe leave the packhorse, but then thought about his need to explore and decided to continue his travels as before, keeping everything with him. He broke camp and started north out of the valley of the Cucharas River. He used a distant white mountain as his landmark and held near the tree line to his west. Although the run-off ravines from the mountains gave him an up and down route to travel, he soon found a game trail within the timber that was easier going. Always observant, he watched for game, Indian sign, and a possible location for his winter quarters, all the while thinking about the wagon train that still bothered him with that uneasy feeling.

It was about mid-afternoon when he spotted the trail at the base of the tall ridge-like white mountain. He reined up and looked at the strange spectacle of the white mountain. It appeared like a long ridge with the white rock on its crest at its forward and highest point, some kind of rock that appeared like an ancient sculpture that had crumbled with its many pieces cascading down the mountainside. Tatum had never seen such a marvel, but he knew this unique sight was only a marvel to him, having never seen the like before. He looked at the trail that followed the creek in the bottom of the narrow valley and followed it with his eyes eastward to find the white snake of a caravan slowly ascending the rising hills.

He reined his mount back into the trees and worked his way higher up the mountainside and deeper in the timber, searching for a promontory like the one he used yesterday when he spotted the train. He ducked and bobbed looking through the branches of the fir and pine until he saw a slight clearing up near a ridge of rock. It was an escarpment that extended away from the trees and would afford him an excellent observation point. He picketed his horses below the rocks and taking his rifle and spyglass, made his way through the slide-rock and to the crest. As he looked it over, he grinned at his choice and walked to the point to take up his vigil.

As he watched, an advance party of several men carrying shovels, axes, and picks walked along the trail, stopping every now and then to clear away and even widen the trail for the wagons that followed. Carson had said this was a trail used by pack trains and even military detachments, but never by wagons although he thought that would happen soon enough. Little did he know how prophetic his words were nor how soon they would become reality. These pilgrims were determined to make their way to the Old Spanish trail, or maybe they were planning on settling somewhere in these mountains. Tatum was disturbed at the thought of settlers encroaching on his newfound territory and hoped they were just passing through but, somehow, he knew that might not be true.

His curiosity prompted him to visually follow the trail upstream to evaluate their progress and the challenges before them regarding clearing the way. Near the crest of the trail and the headwaters of the creek below them, the timber thinned out somewhat and another trail came from behind the white ridge. As he looked he saw some movement and focused his attention to see a group of Indians that he guessed to be Comanche, probably a hunting party, coming from the uphill side and take to the trail that would lead them into the workers from the wagon train. He estimated just over an hour before they spotted one another, and he began to calculate if he had time to warn the pilgrims. He looked to his horses, scurried from his promontory, sliding down the loose shale to the animals. He left the packhorse tethered, loosed his sorrel and swung aboard, reining around to descend the hillside to give the members of the train a warning of the impending attack.

Foregoing any stealth, he rode from the timber to the alarm of the workers that looked up at the charging rider and held their tools as weapons for defense. But recognizing the man as a white man, they relaxed until he arrived. When Tatum reined up beside the men on the trail, he quickly told them of the approaching Indians. "I'm pretty sure they're Comanche, but it looks like there's only about a dozen or so and if you make it back to your wagons, your bigger numbers will probably discourage any attack. At least you'll be armed and can defend yourself."

"Who are you and why should we believe what you're saying," growled one of the men, still holding a pick as a weapon acting like he was ready to attack Tatum.

"Doesn't make any difference who I am, and you can believe me or not. But if you stay here, you're sure to be attacked by a band of Indians that would like nothing more than to hang your scalps from their shields or lances, and then your families would have fewer men to protect them. So, believe me or not, in about a half hour or so you'll find out for yourself. So, what you do is up to you. I've done my duty." He looked at the men, still immobile in disbelief or just unsure of what to do, and Tatum shook his head in frustration and reined around to retrieve his packhorse and fend for himself. As he rode away, he turned back and saw the men walking back to the wagons and he hoped they would make it before the Comanche caught up with them.

As he entered the trees, he thought about his own protection and knew he had left a clear trail in his hurry to descend the mountain to warn the pilgrims. He dropped from his mount, led his sorrel uphill into the trees and tethered him, then returned to his tracks that crossed the game trail. Using his moccasins, he wiped out his prints, scattered dust and pine needles over his tracks to both sides of the game trail, walked back uphill and did the same until his tracks were reasonably obscured well off the path. He knew his impromptu efforts would not completely obliterate signs of his passing and if an experienced tracker was purposely looking for his tracks, he could easily be found. But his concern was for the casual observer to miss any obvious sign and pass on by without alarm.

He returned to his escarpment of observation and took up his spyglass to observe whatever would unfold before him. The workers were barely within sight of the wagons, now circled and straddling the small stream on the last sizable flat at the entrance of the valley where the men had been clearing trail. Suddenly, the war cries and screams of the Comanche gave the men their needed motivation to drop their tools and start running to the wagons. Tatum couldn't help himself as he chuckled at the sight of the panicked men running for their lives and he thought, *maybe next time they'll pay attention when someone tries to warn them.* Most of the men were nearing the wagons but one man, somewhat overweight, trailed far behind and staggered down the trail, arms flailing as he tried hollering for help. But the rest of the men in the work crew were not concerned about anyone but themselves and without their knowing, the fat man fell face down to be overtaken by the Indians who shot arrow after arrow into his body until it resembled a pincushion. One of the warriors dropped from his mount, straddled the body and with practiced moves, took the man's scalp. He stood and chanted his war cry and quickly remounted to join his fellow warriors.

When the Comanche spotted the circled wagon train, they reined up and conferred with one another. Tatum could tell they were arguing and gesticulating toward the wagons, but within moments apparently came to an agreement and took off at a trot behind a couple of knolls that shielded them from the view of the wagons as they moved along the trail back the direction Tatum came from just that morning. *I hope they don't spot my tracks and come after me*, thought the young man, now turning his attention back to the wagon train.

He wasn't near enough to hear what they were saying, but their actions spoke loud enough. Four men were sent to retrieve the body of the man they left behind while others worked to fortify their circle with boxes, barrels and brush stacked between the wagons. They left one opening in the direction of their grazing animals and stationed a couple of men on the nearby knolls to watch for any other attacks. Tatum thought they were doing what was probably best, but he thought they were a bit lax in their preparations. *They are just thinking those few in the huntin' party are all to be concerned about, but I'm thinkin' that bunch is headed to their village and will return with a whole lot more warriors. When they see how many horses these pilgrims have and with all the wagons full of plunder, yeah, they'll bring all their fightin' men for this little set-to*, thought Tatum.

CHAPTER SIXTEEN
DEFENSE

IT WAS A FRUSTRATED AND DISGUSTED TATUM THAT LED HIS packhorse from the trees as he pointed his sorrel toward the circled wagons. He was arguing with himself about his actions but knew he was obligated to do what he could to warn the pilgrims of the dangers they were facing. As he neared the circle, he was stopped by a gruff voice demanding, "Who're you and whatchu want?" Tatum looked to see a somewhat scruffy pot-bellied man with scraggly whiskers and tousled hair trying to escape a floppy hat. Tobacco juice stained his greying whiskers and squinty eyes that glared from under thick eyebrows did little to allay a first impression that this man bullied his way and seldom met with argument. He was a big man, well over six feet, with broad shoulders that strained the seams of a soiled vest and arms that held a scarred Kentucky-style percussion rifle that wavered in the direction of Tatum.

The young man reined up and heard a voice from behind the wagon say, "That's the man what warned us, Cletus!" The big man looked to his left and back at Tatum, "You didn't answer me, boy. Who're you an' whatchu want?" he growled.

Tatum crossed his forearms and rested them on the saddle horn as he leaned forward. He answered, "Well, the Osage call me TatumTatum, the Kiowa call me Long Bow, Carson calls me Tate, but the Comanche and Apache have yet to make my acquaintance, so take your pick."

"Look, boy, I don't need none o' yore smart talk. Keep it up an' I'll have to teach you some manners!"

Tatum looked at the man, sat up and reined his horse around to leave but was stopped when another man shouted, "No! Wait! You came to tell us something, what was it?" Tatum twisted around in his seat and looked back to see another man, dark complexioned with black wavy hair and an unusual cap set on the back of his head. His expression was pleading yet friendly so Tatum responded, "Well, those Comanche that you saw earlier," and was interrupted by the burly bully, "What about 'em? Didn't you see how they turned tail when they saw how many we had?"

Tatum reined back around to face the growing crowd and asked, "Are you the wagonmaster?"

"That's right. Cletus Morgan, now whatchu got to say?"

"Those Comanche didn't turn tail. Their village is back down that valley yonder and, according to Carson, there's eighty or more lodges."

"Yeah, so what? They run, didn't they?" snarled the bully.

"Let him talk, Cletus, it might be important," pleaded one of the crowd.

Tatum waited a moment and started, "Well, I s'pose you probably already figgered this out but those Comanche don't run from anything. All they did was head off to their village to let the rest of 'em know that you've got a lot of horses and women and children. And in their eyes, that's all they need to come back in force to take it all from you."

"You mean they're gonna come back?" asked a woman's voice.

"That's right, ma'am. Now I don't mean to scare you, but the way these Comanche work, they kill all the men, take the women and children and horses and use 'em up and trade 'em to the Comancheros, that's Mexican traders outta Taos and places like that."

The crowd became uneasy and chattering among themselves until the wagonmaster shouted, "Now hold on! We don't know if what this boy is sayin' is true!" and he looked back at Tatum and asked, "Why should we take yore word? You ain't nuthin' but a boy anyway."

"Fine, stay here and wait for 'em. They'd like that."

"Wait, Tate, is that your name?" asked the earlier speaker with the dark hair.

"That's right, and you're ... "

"I'm Vittorio Bertolini and we are travelers with thees train. Iffa whatta you say ees true, what should we do?"

The crowd looked at one another and the bully of a wagonmaster said, "I think we should stay right here, we can fight off them Injuns, we got guns ain't we?"

"Look around," replied Tatum, waving his hand for emphasis. "All around you, there's high ground. From just about any place, the Comanche can rain down arrows and never show themselves. And it'll take them till late tonight or early tomorrow to reach their village, and you could be long gone by then."

"Whatta you mean, long gone?" asked Vittorio.

"If you folks start off right away, send your work crew ahead like you did earlier, only make it a bigger crew, you might be able to top off on the flat at the crest of this pass by morning. That'll at least give you the high ground and a clear field of fire if they were to attack. But with a day's head start, you might even keep goin' and be well away from here 'fore they catch up with you."

"You mean tuck our tails an' run, don'tchu?" snarled the wagonmaster.

"No, I mean protect your women and children," answered Tatum.

"And just what stake do you have in this?"

"None, none at all. Just a clear conscience and knowing I won't have to dig any graves for those young'uns playin' yonder," he said, nodding his head toward a group of children chasing one another.

The crowd started a clamor of talking and shouting as they tried to decide what to do and Tatum caught the eye of Vittorio and motioned him to come near. Tatum leaned down and said, "Look, if you folks decide to move out, move as fast as you can. The worst spot is a couple of switchbacks in the trail a couple of miles up, but if you make it up that hillside, the goin'll be easy after that. I'm goin' back into the trees and up on that rise behind me. I'll watch for any sign of the Comanche and I'll fire a shot in your direction so you'll have warning. I'll follow you at a distance to keep watch and sound the alarm if necessary." He looked at the sky and added, "It's gonna be a clear night; the moon's just waxing past the first quarter so you'll have light enough. Just keep 'em goin' all night long. They can rest after you get to the top."

Vittorio nodded to Tatum and patted him on the leg and answered, "We will get there, you will see, we Italian don't stop."

"Good, good. Remember, your life might depend on it," said Tatum and reined his horse around and started toward the trees. The others were still arguing as he disappeared and as he made his way to the crest of the knoll that overlooked the valley where the wagon was circled, he picketed his horses. Taking his long bow and quiver and his Hawken, he walked to the crest and found a place among some scrub oak brush to take up his watch. It wasn't long until he saw the work crew start up the trail to begin their work in advance of the wagons.

The wagon train had long passed the bend in the trail that was masked by the pines, and Tatum looked to the starlit sky and judged the time to be near midnight. Sound carries in the darkness and he could occasionally make out the clatter of picks and shovels as the men worked to clear and widen the trail for the wagons to follow. When he had scrutinized the trail with his spyglass the day before, he knew the hardest part would be the switchbacks that would climb the hill to the south side of the creek that paralleled the trail. Once they passed the switchbacks, the trail would round the shoulder of the mountain and follow the natural contour of the mountainside and lead them to the top and the crest of the pass. If they made it past the switchbacks by midnight, he thought they would make the park by first light. Tatum planned to stay where he was to watch for the Comanche and try to delay them.

He always enjoyed the night, the many weeks of traveling in the darkness had acquainted him with the creatures of the dark and he smiled as he listened and watched. The cicadas in the flats, the frogs from the creek bottom, the questions from the owls and the high-pitched cries of the bats were all familiar and even comforting sounds of the night. In the distance a pair of coyotes sang their love song and a whippoorwill with it trilling chirp and a nighthawk with its long high-pitched screech gave Tatum the assurance that he was alone on the knoll.

He looked to the east and knew morning's light would soon make silhouettes of the hills so he stood, stretched and walked down to secure his horses to pursue the wagons. He chose to stay high and rode to the top of the ridge that paralleled the valley with the roadway taken by the wagons. A game trail gave passage through the tall fir and spruce that covered the north flanks of the hills facing the white-topped mountain. After an hour of traveling and with daylight covering the timber, he made his way to a clearing that would provide a view of the trail below. As he stepped beside a tall ponderosa, he could see a large band of Indians approaching the previous site of the wagons and he could tell they were not surprised to find the meadow empty; after a short conference, they started up the trail in pursuit of the fleeing wagons.

Tatum strung his bow with his usual step-through action and once the bow was ready, he moved away from the ponderosa to give himself a clear view of the Comanche. He knew he was still protected from the sight of the Indians below by the many treetops before him, but he needed a clear shot for what he planned. He stepped back from the trees, nocked an arrow and stepped into his shot and let the arrow fly. He immediately dropped to a crouch to conceal himself but to still see the effect of his arrow. Suddenly one of the men near the front of the band screamed and clutched at the arrow that pierced his chest and protruded from his back. He fell off his horse as he grasped for the mane but failed. Those beside him looked in the general direction of Tatum but he knew he could not be seen and continued to watch their reaction. The entire band had stopped and dismounted, using their horses as shields and scattered into the brush alongside the trail. Tatum knew the arrow would be confusing to the Comanche; with no tribal markings they would wonder what other bands would be in Comanche lands and take their attention from the wagons.

Tatum mounted up and following the trail, well obscured in the black timber, soon dropped down to cross the dry ravine that fed storm water to the creek below. He pointed his sorrel to the point of the ridge that was rounded by the roadway but he kept off the crest, preferring to stay on the game trail that wound through the buck brush. Before reaching the trail, now widened by the passing wagons, he ground tied his horses and walked through the brush to the crest of the ridge to look back along the trail for any sign of the Comanche.

Using a cluster of juniper for cover, he scanned the valley below and easily spotted the pursuing Indians. He guessed the band to number less than half of the previous number but still numbering over fifty warriors. *Well, let's see if we can cut the numbers down some more,* he thought as he looked for a good firing position. He soon found a tall cluster of brush, stepped beside it and launched another missile of death. Because the group had moved past Tatum's position as they followed the trail of the wagons, this arrow came from above and behind them, but another warrior fell from his horse, alarming his fellow warriors that once again took cover to try to find the attacker. Since it was an arrow, they naturally looked in the distance that would be the common range of the bows they used which would be around one hundred yards maximum. But Tatum's bow had a range well over twice that distance, enabling him to move away without being seen.

As he approached the circle of wagons in the middle of the wide meadow at the crest of the pass, he was pleased to see they had fortified between the wagons and had all their stock within the circle. He waved in answer to the wave of one of the guards that he soon recognized as Vittorio and as he walked his sorrel to the wagon, he was welcomed by the grinning Italian. "Tate, it is good to see you. Did you see any Indians?"

"A few, slowed 'em up a bit, but they might still be comin', 'bout fifty of 'em now," he said as he stepped down. Vittorio had two other men open a passageway for Tatum to bring his horses into the circle and motioned to his wife to get him some food. Tatum smiled at the woman as she motioned for him to sit on the keg beside the wagon and handed him a plate of stew. He was thankful for the food, and wasted little time putting it away. The Indians would just have to wait.

"HERE THEY COME!" SHOUTED THE GUARD THAT STOOD WITH one foot on the lowered wagon tongue. He was looking at the tree line where the trail emerged and pointed at the band of Comanche as they started to spread out at the edge of the wide barren flat that held the wagons. The circle of wagons was well placed atop the slight rise near the center of the wide open flat. With a clear field of fire close to three hundred yards in all directions, the Indians couldn't get near the wagons without coming under fire of the rifles in the hands of the pilgrims. Tatum went to the side of Vittorio as he stood at the rear of a wagon facing the emerging Indians. Vittorio looked at the young man and said, "I'ma very glad you told us to come here. It'sa much better than below," and nodded his head in the direction of their previous camp. "But, that'sa lotta Indians and they don't look ver' happy."

Tatum chuckled at Vittorio's observation and replied, "Ain't none of us lookin' too happy either."

The big wagonmaster walked toward the two men now observing the Indians and said, "Alright, we made it up hyar, now what, mister know-it-all?"

Tatum looked at the brute of a man and replied, "I don't know it all, but I think you did right by movin' up here. If the original bunch had caught you down below, your scalp would be decoratin' some warrior's shield or lance by now."

"What do you mean by that!" growled the wagonmaster.

"That's only 'bout half of 'em," replied Tatum, nodding toward the Indians. He watched as the band split three groups off and sent them to circle around the wagons. The orders for the Comanche were coming from the group that stayed at the edge of the timber by the trail. Tatum continued, "They split their band back down the trail a ways. Seems they thought some other Indian tribe was hornin' in on their territory and they took out after 'em."

The wagonmaster stared at Tatum, not understanding what he meant and started to speak but was stopped when Tatum said, "They're gettin' ready to attack. You might wanna tell your people to get ready and space their shots. The Comanche will try to draw your first shots and while you're reloading, they'll charge with most of their forces." Although Tatum had never endured a charge by this number of Indians, he had listened well to both Rastus and Carson as they shared their knowledge and both men had spoken of the wisdom of the red man.

In Tatum's brief visit with the people of the wagons, he had taken mental note of the rifles and other weapons of the pilgrims. His was the only Hawken among the many rifles held by the rest of the wagons, where others had both percussion and flintlocks and a couple had percussion shotguns. The well-designed Hawken was known to have an effective range of close to four hundred yards, but Tatum had never put it to the test. Now he was thinking that time had come.

Cletus had spread the word among the men to space their

shots and make sure all were not reloading at the same time. But when men are under fire, fear has a way of interfering with rationale and common sense. Tatum noticed several women were beside their men, holding pistols at their sides and ready to assist with the reloading of the weapons. He smiled at the thought of his mother saying, "A woman's place is in the home and she has no business with firearms, ever!" And yet his mother showed bravery beyond most men when she willingly went to the Osage village to tend to those stricken with smallpox, and again when that same plague struck their home town.

At an unseen signal, all four groups of the Comanche started toward the wagons at a full gallop. Screaming their war cries and waving their weapons, it was the first wave to draw the initial fire. Although told to wait until ordered, several of the nervous men fired at the onslaught, causing the others to let loose the first volley from the muzzleloaders. The Indians were weaving back and forth, and lying along the necks of their horses, all to keep the pilgrims from having a clear target.

With the first volley fired, the lull in the shooting caused the Indians to move in closer and send a barrage of arrows flying in search of a target. Screams rose from among the pilgrims as a few were pierced with arrows and others with near misses; the fear rose and panic began to set in among the defenders of the wagons. Tatum had fired, reloaded, and fired again, unseating two charging Comanche, when his attention was drawn to a family at the next wagon. Three children had hidden inside the wagon and a Comanche warrior was climbing into the wagon after them as the oldest girl screamed and kicked at him. Tatum saw the woman of the wagon bending over the prone form of her husband, oblivious to what was happening with her children. Tatum

ran to the fracas and grabbed at the breechcloth of the
warrior as he climbed over the tailgate and as the warrior
turned to face the new threat, Tatum buried his tomahawk in
the attacker's forehead. The scream of the girl and crying of
the other children was momentarily stopped when they saw
the Indian topple from the wagon.

Tatum snatched his tomahawk, wiped it on the breech-
cloth of the dead Comanche, and quickly returned to his
place in the circle of wagons. He raised his Hawken, but saw
the Indians riding away from the circle and return to the far
tree line. He stood on the wagon seat to look at the carnage
before him and counted seven bodies of Comanche, three
dead horses, and one wounded warrior struggling to his feet
to try to flee.

He stepped down and looked around the inside of the
wagon circle and saw what appeared to be four men down
with women tending to them, including the one at the next
wagon, but that woman was just weeping over her dead
husband's body. He saw the wagonmaster moving among the
people and ordering them to get back in their place before
the Indians returned. Tatum turned back to Vittorio and saw
the man looking at a wagon farther around the circle and
back to Tatum, "Go ahead, Vittorio. I'll stay here." Tatum had
rightly judged the man being concerned about his family that
was in the other wagon and that he wanted to ensure they
were alright.

When Vittorio returned with a relieved look on his face,
Tatum excused himself to walk the circle of wagons. At
several of the barricaded spaces, Tatum looked beyond the
wagons to see what the tally might be of downed Indians. As
he finished his count and returned to his place, the wagonmaster strutted up and boasted, "Wal, I guess we showed 'em!
I don't think they'll come back for more, didn't I tell ya'?"

"You might be right. Indians always consider the cost of any battle, and this one cost them. I counted eighteen dead, and three of your men as well. Now, if their leaders consider the cost too great, they might leave after they take the bodies. But, if the idea of vengeance weighs heavy on 'em, they might come back. Reckon we'll just have to wait an' see," surmised Tatum.

"Hummpph, they're gonna tuck their tails 'tween their legs an' run on outta hyar. We showed 'em, stinkin' Injuns!" growled Morgan and walked away, disgusted at Tatum's remarks.

Tatum shook his head and wondered at such a remark as 'stinkin' Injuns' when the man that said it probably hadn't taken a bath in over a month and pushed a tide of stink wherever he went.

Four men were posted as the first rotation of guards while the others tended the animals and made ready for their evening meal. Tatum was asked to join Vittorio's family and was pleased when Vittorio led his family in a prayer of thanksgiving for their safety, provisions, and new friend. It was a hastily prepared meal of spicy venison stew and bread, both of which were greatly enjoyed by Tatum. Vittorio had a pleasant family of four children; the oldest, Rosa, was about the same age as Tatum, and the two boys, Alberto and Luciano, were eleven and nine and the youngest, Anna, was five. While Vittorio and his wife, Gigi, sat at the table with Tatum, the youngsters tended to their chores of cleaning up after the meal and feeding the horses. Tatum smiled at the family activity, thinking about what he had missed after his mother died. His only family being his father with his grief-driven drinking, Tatum had to grow up too fast, his only time with others of his own age being in his father's classes at school.

The thought of his father sobered Tatum and he excused himself after thanking the Bertolini's for the fine meal. He took his turn at guard and after his rotation was done, he found a place for his bedroll near another wagon and was soon sound asleep. But just after midnight, he was stirred from his slumber by some sound beyond the wagons. The gibbous moon was tucked behind a cloud but as Tatum watched, he saw several shadowy figures moving slowly across the flats. He rolled to his belly and pulled the Hawken to his shoulder but held his fire when he realized the Comanche were just taking their dead. He rolled back from his blankets and started around the circle of wagons, wanting to caution the others not to fire and to let the Comanche take their dead. Two of the three remaining guards were snoozing and Tatum let them sleep, and the other guard agreed with Tatum's decision to let the Indians do their work.

By first light, the flats before them were devoid of any sign of Indians. Most of the pilgrims were surprised to learn the Comanche had so quietly removed their dead and were no longer within sight. Gigi Bertolini asked Tatum, "Does that mean they are gone?"

"I'm not sure, ma'am, but I reckon I'll take a ride and check on 'em, just to be sure."

As he was saddling his sorrel, the wagonmaster walked up and snarled, "Now where ya goin'? Leavin' us, huh?"

Tatum looked at the big man that stood too close, trying to intimidate the young man with his size, and continued his work as he answered, "Just gonna go take a look, make sure they're not gatherin' up for another attack."

"I tol' ya they tucked their tails, but you go 'head on, sonny, you'll see I'm right."

Tatum didn't answer but mounted up and reined around to leave through the passageway made by Vittorio. As he passed his friend, Tatum cautioned, "You be sure to put that back, an' don't anybody leave till I get back. If I don't come back, that packhorse and all it's got, is yours," as he motioned toward the horse herd where the bay packhorse stood watching.

"You'll be back!" declared a smiling Vittorio as Tatum rode away.

"IT LOOKS LIKE THEY'VE GONE," EXPLAINED TATUM AS THE crowd from the wagon train gathered around. He had made a scout of the trees along the trail that led to their circle and by all signs, he concluded the entire contingent of Comanche had left the vicinity, probably to return to their encampment on the Cucharas River.

"But do you think they will come back?" asked Vittorio, standing beside Cletus Morgan.

"Hard to say but, based on the sign, I'd say they've gone. If they were to come back, you've got a couple of days to skedaddle," answered Tatum.

"Wal, that's good 'nuff fer me, I say we pack up an' light a shuck outta hyar. We can leave a rear guard just in case, but I think we whupped 'em an' they ain't wantin' no more," proclaimed Morgan. The rest of the crowd seemed to agree and moved away to prepare to leave. Tatum calculated it would take at least two days for the wagons to leave the mountains and reach the valley below, especially with the continuing need of clearing and widening the trail. But that was none of his concern. He was looking forward to being free of all these pilgrims and particularly away from men like Cletus Morgan. Although he enjoyed his time with the Bertolini family, Morgan was the epitome of all that Tatum despised.

He retrieved his packhorse, rigged him with the pack saddle and other gear and led him to the Bertolini wagon to bid his good byes. Mrs. Bertolini was busy packing their possessions into the wagon while Vittorio harnessed their team. Rosa was helping her mother and was the first to see Tatum's approach and flashed him a welcoming smile. Tatum flushed as he dropped his head to check the cinch of the sorrel and looked back up to see Rosa still smiling at him. He looked away as if he was watching Vittorio harness the team, but the father had already seen the interaction between the two and he grinned and started humming some tune from his past.

"Ahh, Tate, I see you have packed your horse and it looks like you are leaving. Are you not coming with us through these mountains?" asked a grinning Vittorio. "I'm sure my entire family would feel safer if you came along," he added as he glanced at his embarrassed daughter.

Tatum saw what the Italian father was doing and grinned in response but said, "No, Vittorio. I am not coming along. I'm sure your family will be safe, and I have much to do before the end of summer."

"Ahh, my friend, you will be missed. It has been good to have you with us. Perhaps you will visit us again, no?"

"Perhaps, but you will probably be long gone before I can get back. Besides, you told me you wanted to get the vines planted in the soil of California, and you have a long way to go."

"Si, si, but a journey is always better when you have friends with you," explained Vittorio. Gigi, Vittorio's wife, came from behind the wagon with her arms outstretched and declared, "You cannot leave without a hug from mama!" Tatum smiled and waited as she came to him and wrapped her arms around him and held him close. "You have saved our lives, you are now a part of my family," she stated as she stepped back and looked up at the flushing face of Tatum. She looked back at Rosa and to Tatum and said, "We will all miss you. You must come see us again and don'ta you forget!" she declared very seriously and then let a smile paint her face as she hugged him again.

Tatum reached out to shake Vittorio's hand, turned and swung aboard his sorrel, looked at Rosa and smiled as he tipped his hat, and reined around to leave. As he rode from the train, he turned around in the saddle to see Rosa standing on the wagon seat and waving. He lifted his hat and waved back, then dropped back into his saddle and gigged his sorrel toward the trees.

As he entered the trees, Tatum stopped, stood in his stirrups and sucked in a deep breath, reveling in the smell of pines and the clean fresh air of the mountains. He was glad to be alone again; he savored the freedom and solitude that was his as he roamed the mountains. This had been his goal, to reach the mountains and explore and live within the realm of the wilderness, to learn in the greatest classroom as he traveled, secure in the hand of his God.

From the flats atop the pass where the wagons had stopped, Tatum sighted four towering granite-topped mountains still holding a mantle of snow directly to the west that stood as the sentinels of the wide valley beyond. To the north, he also saw the magnificent Sangre de Cristo range that seemed to march into the distance beyond where his eyes could see, and he hoped he could circle the sentinel of four and cross over the Sangres into the valley of the San Luis. If not, he would come back to the south side and follow the trail of the wagons.

There were towering fir and spruce intermingled with the long-needled ponderosa that blanketed the eastern slopes of the massive mountains. Several game trails crisscrossed the mountainside, but Tatum chose the most-traveled one that hugged the contours of the mountain and led uphill at an easy grade. When the trail broke from the black timber into the occasional grassy park, Tatum would step from his mount and let the horses graze while he surveyed the country. He often used his spyglass to aid his exploratory scans as he looked for the elusive cave or overhang as suggested by Carson.

His journey continued and took him through a large grove of quakies or aspen that shook their leaves at the intruder like a scolding schoolmarm. Tatum noticed the difference in the smell of the aspen and that of the pines, realizing he could detect many different odors, and he began to pay close attention, not just to what he saw but what he heard and the many odors that seemed to taunt him for recognition. As he considered this new revelation, he heard breaking branches below him and looked down the hillside to see several elk breaking their way through the thick cluster of aspen. They crossed below him and turned uphill, vanishing in the thick timber beyond. He immediately detected the different smell and mentally marked it as elk, surprised that he recognized the unique smell of the royalty of the woods.

Pleased with himself and this most recently learned lesson, he gigged his mount forward as they approached the large shoulder that came from the mountain above, believing this was the last obstacle before he would find a crossing of the Sangres. The trail continued through the black timber and worked its way around the point of the shoulder. As they neared the point, the sorrel jerked his head up, ears forward and snorted. He stopped suddenly and began to toss his head in protest as his shoulders began to nervously shake. Tatum looked at the bay to see the big packhorse showing the same signs of nervousness. Both horses were prancing and resisted any urging to move forward. Distracted by the action of the horses, Tatum missed his first cue but when it came, he recognized the biting stench as the cause of the fear in the horses. He reined the sorrel around and passed beside the bay before pulling the lead to turn the packhorse around. Tatum moved back down the trail about fifty yards, stopped and dismounted. He tethered the horses to a nearby sapling, retrieved his Hawken from the scabbard and started back up the trail to see what had been the cause for alarm.

The nearer he came to the crest of the shoulder, the stronger the scent, and he dropped to a crouch before he reached the crest. He carefully moved to the edge, bellied down and with just the top of his head showing, he looked to see a big sow grizzly and two cubs burrowing among the slide rock for some mysterious tidbit. He watched as the massive beast turned over slide rocks, digging beneath each one, finding something that she would snatch with her mouth, and move on to another. The two cubs busied themselves mimicking their mother, but less successful. The sow was definitely the source of the bitter scent and Tatum watched her slowly work her way up the broad expanse of moss-covered slide rock. He looked below the slide area where many of the large boulders had tumbled into the aspen below and saw no evidence of a trail that had apparently ended at the slide.

Suddenly the big sow straightened up and barked a growl as she twisted around to find her cubs. Both were nearby but something else had garnered her attention and Tatum realized he was the source of her concern. He crabbed back away from the ridge and trotted to his horses, repeatedly looking back to see if he was being chased. He grabbed the leads of

the horses, swung aboard and dug heels to the ribs of the
sorrel and the horses willingly responded and cantered back
down the trail leaving the grizzly to her cubs.

When he felt they were far enough away from the bear,
Tatum reined up and twisted in his seat to look back up the
trail for any sign of pursuit. With no sounds and no smells,
he relaxed and dropped back into his seat and gigged his
sorrel to move. As he thought about this recent lesson from
the wilderness school, he grinned and even laughed at
himself, remembering the sudden case of fear when he
thought the grizzly was going to come after him. He reached
down and stroked the neck of the sorrel, thankful he had
warned his rider of the danger. Another lesson learned:
always pay attention to your horses.

He followed a small stream uphill and found his campsite
for the night. It was in a small secluded clearing at the foot of
a thicket of aspen that filled a wide ravine and crawled up the
mountainside. The small park-like setting offered a comfortable blanket of grass for his bedroll and ample dry wood
nearby for his campfire. After unsaddling, he picketed the
horses within reach of the water and grass, gathered his firewood and started his coffee.

It was dark when he finished his supper and stretched out
in his bedroll. With hands locked behind his head, he looked
at the stars, contemplating the previous days with the wagon
train and meeting new friends, and grinned at the memory
of Rosa. He considered the days ahead and wondered about
the progress of the wagons and if there had been any other
run-ins with Indians. He hoped not, and included them in his
prayers for the night before dropping off to a well-earned
rest.

The nearby screech of a nighthawk brought him instantly
awake, but he did not move except to look toward the horses
and see if they were alarmed. Still standing hipshot and

quiet, they paid no attention to the nighthawk or the many other noises of the night. He looked heavenward and judged the time to be near daybreak and rolled to his side to try for a bit more sleep. But his mind began to work and knowing that once his thoughts started their parade through his mind, sleep would not be found. He rolled from his blankets and walked to the spring-fed stream, splashed water on his face and neck and straightened to welcome the day.

His chosen route for the day would take him around the southern flanks of the sentinel mountains and give him ample opportunity for exploring the upper reaches of the timbered slopes. He often stopped to search the rocky crags for cave openings or an overhang that would be suitable for converting into a winter shelter. He enjoyed the discovery of different animals and chuckled when he spotted his first whistle pig. The fat marmot sat on a large boulder surveying his domain and was startled by the intruder, dropped to all fours and whistled a warning to his fellow rock dwellers and disappeared through a crack that Tatum was certain would not let him pass. To his surprise, the chubby-looking rodent slipped easily away.

As he stopped for the mid-day break to give his horses time to roll and graze, he used his spyglass to survey his surroundings. While examining a protruding cliff face, a movement caught his eye and he watched a pair of white rumps disappear behind an outcropping. He held his glass on the rocks and saw the two bighorn sheep, both rams, walk to a promontory and lay down yet with heads high as they watched the mountainside below them. They were an impressive sight and the first seen by Tatum. He remembered what his father often said, "Part of the joy of learning is to share with others your knowledge." He wished his father was here to share his latest lesson from his wilderness education.

Later in the afternoon, he stopped in another clearing and let his horses graze while he withdrew his spyglass and scanned the slopes above. Paying close attention to any rocky areas, still searching for a shelter, he took his time surveying the towering mountain. From this location he could see the massive granite face of the largest of the four sentinel mountains. A few specks in the distance seemed to move but were too far away to identify. The rocky face of the mountain yielded no prospects of caves or other shelters and he turned his attention below him. When he lowered the spyglass, he sat down and took a few moments to just take in the magnificent panorama before him. He was amazed at the distances he could see in the clear mountain air. To the south were the Spanish Peaks that were two or three days travel away, and back to his left the plains stretched out beyond the length of his eyesight. But in the distance, he thought he could make out the location of Bent's Fort. As he looked to his right, he saw the valley widen into what he thought was the mouth of the San Luis valley, and he thought of the wagon train and wondered how far they had traveled since he left them just two days ago...and if Rosa was thinking about him as often as he was thinking about her.

CHAPTER NINETEEN
RETURN

THE SUN WAS JUST PUSHING THE PINK ABOVE THE HORIZON when Tatum poured his first cup of coffee. It had been a restless night and he didn't know why. That same feeling of uneasiness like he had when he first saw the wagon train was once again nagging at him. He was learning to heed his premonitions, if that's what they were. His pa had often told him that, "We have a sixth sense that gets dimmed with the noise of civilization but you should always pay attention to it; it might save your bacon someday." He tossed the dregs of his coffee to the side and finished packing his gear to start off for the day. Maybe he would find the wagon train and ease his mind as to any trouble. He was sure it wasn't just a want-to regarding seeing Rosa again. They hadn't even talked, just smiled and waved at each other, but there was something about that girl. He grinned at the thought and mounted up.

He still rode the trail that hung on the shoulder of the sentinel mountains making its way through the dark timber and breaking out every so often into grassy parks. His first clear view of the valley below prompted him to stop and take some time to examine the trail for the wagons. He was seated on a grey barkless log when a patch of white caught his eye. He swung his spyglass to see what it was. Wagons! But there were only a few, four of them; where were the rest? He rested his elbows on his knees to steady the glass and scanned as much of the valley as he could see but there were no other wagons. When he looked back at the four, he saw movement of people and the horses were picketed near the trees. They were parked near the trail where it entered the San Luis valley between the trail and the tree line. Not a good defensive position if need be, but it appeared they were close to the water. As he watched, he also calculated the distance and figured it would take a couple of hours to get there. But he determined to go and find the reason for their separation from the rest of the train.

He crossed the roadway and entered the trees, choosing to approach the wagons from the tree line instead of following the main trail. He didn't want some trigger-happy pilgrim taking a pot shot at him. As he neared the site of the wagons, he stopped and looked through the trees at their campsite. It appeared that two women were tending the cook fire, some children were playing in the clearing beyond the wagons, one man stood leaning against a wagon and watching the women while another was busy near the picketed horses. He recognized Mama Bertolini at the cook fire and one of the children was their youngest daughter, but he thought there should be more people around.

He called out, "Hello the camp," and watched as the women stood and the man by the wagon reached for his rifle. "I'm comin' in, if it's alright," said Tatum as he dismounted and started toward the camp, leading his horses. He was instantly recognized by Mrs. Bertolini who put her hand to her mouth and then told the others. The man at the wagon with the rifle lowered it to the ground and watched Tatum approach. Mama Bertolini walked out to meet him and greeted him with a hug and said, "Oh, Tate, I'ma so glad to see you. We've got troubles, ummhumm, troubles."

They walked side by side as Tatum asked, "What kind of troubles, Mama?"

"Sick, so many, sick. Maybe cholera, I dunno, but they sick," she said, shaking her head.

"Is that why the others left you behind?"

"Yes, they thinka we make ever'body sick. Said we could catch up later."

"Well, how many are sick?" asked Tatum.

"Uh, lemme see, there'sa three men, two offa da' women, anna three children."

Tatum had heard about cholera and read about it in his father's books and even in a newspaper from back east. Some thought it had to do with the drinking water but no one was sure. He knew it to be a killer and a fast-acting illness. He asked Mama, "Has anybody, uh, you know, has anybody died?" afraid of the answer.

"No, nobody, just ver' sick in belly, and hot, and pain in head. They really sick."

He looked around for Vittorio and not seeing him asked, "Vittorio?"

Mama Bertolini nodded her head, sadness and fear showing in her eyes. "Maybe you should not stay. You could get sick, too."

He shook his head and replied, "No, I'll help out if I can. I'll picket my horses and be right back." He led the horses to the picket line with the others and nodded to the man nearby who looked up at Tatum and smiled, reaching out to shake hands.

"I am Giuseppe LaBella. I'ma glad you came back," he said, nodding to Tatum all the while. Tatum shook his hand, nodded and replied, "Well, hopefully I can help, but I sure don't know how."

The wind changed directions and Tatum got a whiff of the stench from beyond a cluster of sage, looked that direction and saw a man standing and stretching the galluses over his shoulders and start tottering to return to the wagon. It was Vittorio. The young man walked to the side of his friend and offered his shoulder to help him back to the wagon. A weak smile spread across Vittorio's face as he said, "This is bad. I hope you don't get it."

"Me, too, but I think I'll be alright. Maybe I can help out a mite."

Tatum began thinking about what he had read regarding cholera; the symptoms were severe diarrhea with watery stools and vomiting. He also remembered that many died within hours of developing the disease. He asked Vittorio, "Uh, when you went just now, was it watery?"

"Si, si."

"Was it the color of rice water, you know, milky white?"

"No, no, but it smelled bad, I puked more. Whooeee, if I wasn't sick before, that would make me sick," he declared. Tatum helped him up into the wagon and said, "You get some rest, if you can."

"Si, but my head an' my back, they hurt. And my belly, too," he moaned as he crawled to his bedroll.

Tatum walked to the campfire where Mama had seated herself on a stool to watch over the cooking. He squatted beside her and asked, "Mama, the others that are sick, do they all have the runs?"

She thought a moment and looked at the young man and replied, "No, no, but they all have been, uh, you know," and she mimicked someone vomiting.

"Have they been hot and have a lot of pains?"

She furrowed her brow as she looked at the young man, then thought for a moment and said, "I think so, but I will check on them to see." She stood and started for the nearest wagon. Tatum was remembering the time with his mother when she went to the Osage village and tended those stricken with smallpox. When the word spread about the epidemic, the village of Cape Girardeau counted itself fortunate to have a doctor that knew about smallpox. He came from Massachusetts and had insisted on the children all being vaccinated with a new serum that was called cowpox. Some of those that were vaccinated became ill, including Tatum, but none as ill as those in the village and none of them died. Tatum's mother had also helped nurse those of the Cape that were stricken and, eventually, she also took ill and died. After losing his mother, Tatum learned all he could about the dreaded disease that took her life, wanting to understand what he could and why his mother would give up her life to help others, leaving him behind.

When Mama returned, she looked at Tatum and said, "I think all of the sick have had a fever and have, uh, you know," and again mimicked vomiting.

"Vomited?" asked Tatum. "What about pains," and he motioned to his head, back and stomach.

"Si, si. Is it this cholera?"

"Maybe, maybe not. We'll see in a few days. Just do what you can."

He stood and walked away from the wagons, doing what his pa used to call a *"Thinking walk."* He strolled a short distance, reached down and snatched a shoot of foxtail, put the stem in his mouth and held to the opposite end, thinking about the symptoms of smallpox and what these people might be facing. He also thought about the others in the now departed wagon train and if any of those were infected. But he returned his thoughts to this small group of Italian immigrants and their dream of establishing a vineyard in California to grow their grapes and make their wine. Dreams that might never come to pass.

CHAPTER TWENTY
SICKNESS

THE AFTERNOON OF HIS THIRD DAY OF SICKNESS, VITTORIO crawled from the wagon and walked, although somewhat feebly, to the cook fire to the surprise of his wife. She stood and looked at her husband, smiled and held her arms wide to give him a hug. He walked to her, smiled down at her and they embraced one another. She said, "So, you're-a feeling better, eh?"

"Yes, I am, and I'm hungry, too," replied Vittorio, motioning to the simmering stew in the pot hanging over the fire. Mama Bertolini was the only one at the cook fire; the other woman had taken ill and retreated to her wagon, joining her husband. She said, "There are only a few of us to eat. Only Giuseppe LaBella and Adriana Magnani and Chiara Valturri and a couple of the children have not been sick. Everybody else is sick. But, maybe they getta better like a you?"

"Tate?" asked Vittorio.

"No, Tate no sick. He strong boy, over by horses," she nodded her head in the direction of the horses, now loose and grazing on the grasses. Tatum was watching the animals, sitting and leaning against a ponderosa.

As the day wore on, several of those that were the first to take ill came from their bedrolls looking a little haggard but all reporting they were feeling better. The somber mood of the camp seemed to be lifting and the evening meal saw many of the four families gathered for their first real meal in a couple of days. Tatum looked around the circle and considered the people that he had befriended. All good, hardworking folks that shared a dream of a new life in the fabled California. Although the distant land was still a part of the lands claimed by Mexico, it was said to have fertile soil and endless sunshine. But Tatum was concerned about what might really be ailing these folks and had prayed for them and did whatever he could. Now as he looked around he asked Vittorio, "So, where you folks came from, were you church-goers?"

He had seen Mama Bertolini as she sat near the fire and fingered the beaded necklace she carried in her apron pocket and thought she was praying, but wasn't sure.

Vittorio looked at his friend and said, "Si, we are all good Catholics," nodding his head at the others around the circle.

Tatum looked up at the others and asked, "Well, I don't know much about Catholics, but let me ask you. If you were to die, you know, with an illness or Indian attack or whatever, are you sure about Heaven?"

Vittorio smiled and said, "I said we are Catholics, and the church teaches us to pray and go to church and be good people, and if we do good, then we hope to go to Heaven."

Tatum looked at his friend and around the circle at the others who were looking at him and nodding at what Vittorio had spoken. He couldn't help but think that if he was right about smallpox, most, if not all these folks could be dead within a week. He looked back at Vittorio and said, "But

I'm not talking about church 'cuz there ain't no church out here," waving his hand toward the wide valley before them. "See Vittorio, I read the Bible a lot, and what I know is, it never talks about havin' to be a good church goer to make it to Heaven. But it does tell us that we need to be born again."

"I have heard of that, but I don't know what *born again* means."

"It says in John 3:3, *Except a man be born again, he cannot see the kingdom of God.* It goes on to say that is to be born of water, the first time, and of the Spirit, the *again* time. And He explains in Romans that we just need to ask Him for that free gift of eternal life *Romans 6:23* and we'll live forever in Heaven with Him."

"You mean it's not the church?"

"Well, church is alright, and needful for folks, sure, but the Bible says it's faith in Jesus and if we believe with all our heart *Romans 10:9-10* and ask for that gift, He is faithful to give it to us. That's what He meant in John 14:6 *I am the way, the truth, and the life: no man cometh unto the Father, but by me.*"

Vittorio looked at Tatum and around the circle at the others who were very still and listening to the young man. Giuseppe LaBella sat next to his wife, Luciana, and squeezed her hand and then asked Tatum, "How do we ask for that gift?"

"Just pray, that's all, just pray a simple prayer and ask for it. If you like, I'd be glad to lead you all in a prayer and those of you that want to ask for that gift, just pray along with me."

They looked at one another, and several nodded their heads and looked back at Tatum. Giancarlo Valturri said, "I would like to do that." Others, Chiara, Giancarlo's wife, and the Magnanis nodded their heads and agreed. Tatum said, "Alright, how 'bout we just bow our heads and I'll pray and if you want to, just pray with me." He looked around the circle and saw most everyone bowing their heads and he started,

"Father in heaven, you've been mighty good to us and we're thankin' you for that. But now we're needful, Father, these folks want to make sure of Heaven as their home and together we're asking you for that free gift of eternal life you promised in your Word. God, forgive us for our sins, and come into our hearts and save us. And God, go with us in the days to come 'cuz we sure need you. In Jesus name we pray, Amen." Tatum heard several of the others as they prayed along with him and now they echoed his Amen. He looked to see several upturned faces smiling at him and Sergio Magnani spoke for them when he said, "We thank you, Tate, thank you." Rosa smiled at Tatum and he dropped his head as his face flushed. He could talk to just about anyone about anything, but for some reason she left him tongue-tied.

As they finished their meal, there was a lighter mood as the group believed the sickness had passed. Even though they were weak and not ready to face the task of moving the wagons, they were hopeful they could soon return to their journey. Tatum listened as they talked about the old country and their hopes for the land and dreams for their families, and his heart was heavy with what he expected they would really be facing come tomorrow. If he was right, Vittorio, the first to take ill, would also be the first to show the rash that was the precursor of the actual pox of the disease. Tatum knew he was not in danger because of his vaccination but everyone in this group would be, and perhaps none would survive.

CHAPTER TWENTY-ONE
STRUGGLE

THE FIRST LIGHT OF DAY BROUGHT TATUM TO THE COOK FIRE among the wagons. He already had his own coffee and biscuits for breakfast at his own fire near the picketed horses. He chose to have his bedroll near the picket line, trusting the horses to warn of any danger. As he came to the fire, he saw Vittorio and Mama Bertolini sitting side by side and enjoying the first light of day together; he smiled at their closeness recalling his own parents and their times of intimacy. He found a seat on a large rock that had been used before and looked into the flames wondering what the day would bring. He looked up at Vittorio and the light of the fire reflected off his complexion as he grinned back at Tatum.

"How ya' feelin' this mornin', Vittorio?" asked Tatum.

"Ehh," and held his hand flat before him and wiggled it back and forth, "But, come Dio comanda, whatever God wants."

Tatum looked at his friend, cocked his head to the side as if to get a better look and noticed Vittorio's face as the man scratched at his cheek. It was then that Tatum detected the redness of his face that told of a rash. Tatum stood and walked to his friend, and said, "Let me see," as he pulled the collar of Vittorio aside to see the rash had spread down his neck and to his shoulder. He reached for the man's sleeve and pushed it back to see the rash was also on his forearms. Vittorio looked questioningly at his friend and said, "It is but a rash, no? Probably from the weeds or something?"

Tatum returned to his seat and placed his elbows on his knees and looked to Vittorio and Mama and said, "No, my friend, I'm afraid you have smallpox."

Mama put her hand to her mouth and with wide eyes looked at her husband and back at Tatum and asked, "Are you sure? How do you know?"

"Well, we won't be absolutely sure for a while yet, but I'm pretty sure. I lost my mother to smallpox. I got a vaccination against it but she tended to several folks before she got it and lost her fight. When that happened, I learned all I could about it and even saw it take some folks in my hometown. You see, it starts with the sickness like you had," nodding to Vittorio, "and you get better for a day or so, then the rash comes, and shortly the rash turns into abscesses that will break open and scab over, if . . . " and dropped his gaze to his feet.

"Is there anything we can do?" asked Mama, hopefully.

Tatum looked back up at her and shook his head as he said, "No, nothing more you can do but make 'em comfortable." He looked at Mama and said, "Chances are you'll come down with it soon." Vittorio looked at his wife and they hugged one another, and Mama started sobbing into her husband's shoulder.

Mama looked to Tatum as she asked, "Will anyone, uh, uh, live?"

"Some do, but there's no way of knowing. I'm sorry, Mama."

She wrung her hands and putting both palms to her cheeks, she said, "Piove sul bagnato," which was to say, when it rains it pours.

Tatum looked around the circle and saw others starting for the fire. He stood and gathered several containers and canteens and said, "I'm gonna fetch some fresh water," and walked away from the circle. When he returned, it was evident that Vittorio had told the others what to expect and they looked at Tatum with sad countenances, dropping their heads and turning away.

The first day of the pox was the most difficult. As different ones developed the rash and others started showing abscesses, the pain and discomfort were complicated by the fear of what was to come. Most knew that survival was rare, but not impossible and each one hoped for that rare chance at life. Several fingered their beads and muttered prayers, others stared hopelessly at the cloudless blue sky. Those that had yet to be afflicted helped the others to their bedrolls and sought to make them as comfortable as possible. Tatum tended to those that were already showing abscesses and gave them water and did what he could. As he looked around, he heard the whimpers of the younger children as they asked the inevitable question, "why?" and not receiving a satisfactory answer, lapsed into jags of crying. He cautiously walked from one patient to another, checking on the symptoms and condition of each one. He shook his head as he thought that he was doing exactly what his mother had chosen to do, but he had never thought of himself as some kind of healer or doctor. But he didn't see that he had any choice in the matter. He thought, *When I dreamed about coming to the mountains, this sure wasn't what I was thinkin'.*

The next morning, Tatum took stock of how many were sick and what would be needed for the day. He had already noticed the meat supply was gone and they would need some fresh meat for any kind of broth or stew for the many that were down. Mama Bertolini, still on her feet and tending to the others, was assisted by Isabella Valturri, the oldest daughter of Giancarlo, and Caterina LaBella, Giuseppe's daughter. Sergio Magnani was tending the horses with his son, Aldo, by his side. Tatum went to Mama and said, "I'm going to go get us some fresh meat, maybe an elk or a couple o' deer. But we need plenty for these folks," nodding his head toward the wagons and the bedrolls beneath.

"Si, we do. You have done much for us, an' we are ver' thankful," she said as she touched him on his arm.

"Ah, just doin' what's right, that's all, Mama."

She smiled at the tall youth before her and motioned with her hand for him to leave. As he walked away, she turned to Caterina and said, "That man's a saint, that's what he is, a saint."

Caterina nodded her head in agreement and walked back toward the wagon that held her sick mother.

Tatum crossed the trail and headed to the timber mantle of the sentinel mountains. He had stashed his packs back in the trees near the picketed horses, and now led the big bay packhorse with an empty pack saddle in hopes of loading him down with fresh meat. Since he had seen several elk in the black timber and aspen groves, he hoped to get one and maybe even get a shot at one of those bighorn sheep. He breathed deeply of the pine-scented air and pushed his sorrel to the game trail higher up the slope.

As mid-day approached, Tatum had seen nothing but tracks and other signs of animals but nothing to take for meat. He thought, *Track soup and sign stew never fed anybody!*

The game trail held a considerable number of fresh tracks and he decided to keep following. The trail led around the point of a long ridge that came from high up the side of the mountain and dropped to the other side into a wide draw filled with aspen. Tatum reined up and watched for any movement or other sign of nearby game. He lifted his head and took a big whiff of mountain air, testing for elk. He thought he caught something and stood in his stirrups for a better look. On the far side of the wide draw, he saw movement. He dropped from his saddle with Hawken in hand and looked again in the direction of the movement. He saw brown, thinking he had spotted some elk. He led his horses into the trees to a somewhat level area of the trail, tethered them and started off on foot in pursuit of the elk.

Choosing each step carefully, he stealthily worked his way through the quakies well above the feeding elk. He topped out on the next ridge and over the edge, planning on working his way closer to the elk on the opposite side of the ridge from them and when near, he would move back up to the top, locate them and take his shot. He slowly and cautiously walked below the ridge and downhill. When he was where he thought he was even with the elk, he started up the ridge. Suddenly, the entire bunch of elk exploded over the ridge in his direction and he quickly dropped to one knee, taking the only shot offered. He fired and watched a sizable cow elk stumble, catch herself, take three more steps and fall forward to crumble in a heap. Then he had a thought, *Now, what spooked them?* He looked above him at the crest of the ridge and waited for something to appear but when nothing showed, he walked to the ridge for a look-see beyond. There was nothing that he could see that would have spooked the elk, but he rationalized that just about any kind of noise or disturbance of any kind, harmless though it may be, could alarm wild animals that are only concerned about survival.

Within the hour, Tatum was leading his loaded packhorse and sitting astride his sorrel and bound for the wagons. He wasn't anxious to return to the middle of all the sickness, but he knew the people needed him and he gigged his horse along the trail. It would be at least mid-afternoon before he made it back to the wagons.

When the afternoon sun splashed on his face, Tatum shielded his eyes from the glare. He had just cleared the timber and looked down the slope toward the wagons. The first thing that caught his eye was the smoke, too much smoke, and he realized the wagons were on fire.

He dug heels into the sorrel's ribs and leaned along his neck as the long-legged sorrel lurched into a full gallop. The big horse jumped and slid down the slope, packhorse in tow, and kicked up a cloud of dust at they crossed the trail and followed the timber line to the wagons. He reined back on the sorrel, causing it to drop his haunches into a sliding stop as Tatum jumped off before he stopped. With his Paterson Colt in hand, he ran to the wagons, seeing several arrow-riddled bodies prone near the wagons. One wagon that held the vines smoldered near the tailgate but had not caught full fire. He quickly looked inside, saw no one, and ran from wagon to wagon, shielding his face from the flames. He tried to pull the canvas down from the hoops, but jerked his hand back from the flames. He saw bodies inside and beneath the wagons and began counting and trying to identify who was in the wagons or nearby.

When he completed his count, as near as he could tell there were four missing, all women. Adriana Magnani, Rosa Bertolini, and the two LaBella girls, Caterina and Valentina. Vittorio had burned in the wagon and Mama had been shot through with arrows. The others had met the same fate and now the task of burying them all fell to Tatum. He caught his horses and took them to the site of the picket line, now devoid of animals. He found a shovel in the vine wagon and started digging the graves for his friends. He knew he would have to go after those that took the women, but that would have to wait.

CHAPTER TWENTY-TWO
SEARCH

WITH EVERY TURN OF THE SPADE, MEMORIES FLOODED OVER Tatum. Memories of his mother and father, and memories of each of those whose graves he dug. Children, suffering from the ravages of smallpox and not understanding their suffering, having to die such a horrible death as fire. Families with dreams that turned into nightmares. Hopes of a new tomorrow quashed into ashes that would soon mingle with the dust of other wagons carrying more people that would face similar ends. But as he carried the bodies, wrapped in remnants of blankets and clothing, he thought that perhaps this death was more merciful than the drawn-out agonies of smallpox. They died as they lived, together in love, life and death. He fashioned one large cross and carved simply, "Four families with dreams." A large boulder that sat at the side served as an additional marker upon which he scratched the family names. Around the mass grave, he planted the vines from the wagon, vines that were to be their vineyard that would now probably wither and die. He thought it was as if he was burying their dreams with them.

The sun had just dropped behind the western mountains,

yet the sky was filled with clouds painted orange and gold by the setting sun. Tatum walked to the stream and used his bar of lye soap to scrub the black of the fire and the stench of death from his buckskins and body. He looked to the sky and guessed he had a couple of hours before the waxing moon would give enough light for travel. He would use that time for rest and then he would begin his search.

He savored the night; darkness was his domain. It was when he was alone with the nocturnal creatures that he felt more at home, comfortable with friends and familiar with the dim shadows and muted lights of the night. He embraced the darkness like a comforting blanket and he breathed deep of the night air. It was no challenge to follow the trail of a dozen warriors and ten stolen horses. He knew the captive women were probably mounted on the stolen horses, but he knew he could track them even in the blackest night.

He remembered the valley of the Cucharas River and believed the Comanche had their camp somewhere near or in that valley that he had used as a camp before he met the wagon train. He thought about his first experience in the mountains when he rode up the slopes of the Spanish Peaks and his invigorating experience when he looked around and saw farther than ever before. It was during that first foray that he explored the Cucharas Valley, or part of it, and when he first saw the Comanche, he knew they came from that direction. Now, as he followed their trail, he believed their village and the captives would be found somewhere in that valley.

He gave the sorrel his head and enjoyed the creak of the leather, the shuffling gait of the gelding with an occasional clatter of hoof against stone, and the usual sounds of the night. The trail followed a narrow brush-lined creek in the bottom of a wide ravine that cut its way through the mountains. The gravel bottom, sandy in places, was the path of spring run-off but now held little water in the chuckling creek winding down to the stream that was the water source for the wagons. With the increasing moonlight, a few deer could be seen grazing on the stream side grasses and lifted their heads to view the visitors but, sensing no danger, continued their grazing until Tatum came nearer. The smell of man would cause the deer to bounce away as if their legs were coiled springs. Coyotes would slink away at first sight while nighthawks would circle overhead, watching the intruders to their domain.

The sliver of moon dropped toward the horizon when Tatum rode from the trees into a wide open grassy park. The stream he followed had forked, but he followed the trail of the Comanche that sided the south fork that now led into the park. He left the trail to ride near the tree line, preferring not to make himself so visible, even in the fading moonlight. The park narrowed as the trail neared the tree line where Tatum rode. As it appeared the grassy meadow ended, he chose to make camp.

Before he left the wagons, Tatum deboned the elk he downed for the people of the wagons and knew he would need to smoke whatever meat he would keep. It would be more meat than he could use but, if needed, it could also be used as barter. Tatum was thinking of the captives and had no idea what it would take to free the women, but he wanted to be as prepared as possible. With willow racks and alder for the smoke, he began his work at first light. The fire was well placed under the long limbs of a ponderosa that would dissipate the smoke and he had enough alder to feed the coals for the day. He would slumber near the fire and the horses, allowing access to both the horses for their warnings and the fire that would need to be fed.

It was anything but a restful day. Although he did snooze at every opportunity, he knew it would be sometime before he could truly sleep without concern for his welfare, perhaps never. With packs full, he pointed the sorrel to the trail by the rising moonlight. The dark timber swallowed the trail but the path was still easy to follow. He came to the signs of the first camp of the Comanche and stopped to examine the tracks. As he thought, the warriors had plundered the wagons as well as taking the captives, and he knew things like blankets and clothing could harbor the smallpox and would pass the disease to anyone that handled them. With the images of his friends suffering from the disease, he didn't want that for anyone, even the Comanche. And he knew the Indians, with no natural immunity, could have their entire village wiped out by the disease. But what could he do, one man against possibly hundreds of warriors?

He took to the trail again, ever vigilant for any sign of the village or warriors that might be left behind to watch their backtrail. Before midnight, the trail broke from the thick timber to the valley of the Cucharas River and Tatum once again stayed near the tree line. He knew even in the dim light of the stars and quarter moon, he could be silhouetted in the flats near the river and he chose to use the dark shadows of the timber to hide his movement. He rode slowly and as quietly as possible, preferring to move near the pines with the soft needles to dampen any sound. As he watched the creek bottom, a shadow moved from the willows and Tatum reined up. He slid from the saddle, Hawken in hand, and watched. It was a lone horse but with a lead dangling from his neck and causing him to stumble as he stepped on it. Tatum quietly led his mounts back into the trees, tethered them, and returned to the shadows of the tree line.

Either this was the mount of a rear guard or one of the captured horses that had broken away. Tatum waited, dropped to one knee as he watched, uncertain if this was just a loose horse or the bait in a trap. The loose horse dropped his head to graze and as Tatum estimated the distance to be more than a hundred yards, he knew his own deep shadow cover would obscure him from the view of anyone. But he remained still, breathing slowly and watching. With his eyes accustomed to the darkness and the light of the clear starlit night, he could see anything but that in the deep shadows. As he watched, having waited almost a half hour, a part of the shadow separated itself to become the stealthy figure of a Comanche warrior. He walked slowly to the horse, took the trailing lead rope and led the animal back to the thick willows by the creek. Had Tatum not spotted the horse earlier, he would have ridden within easy bowshot of the concealed warrior.

Tatum rose to his feet and slowly moved back into the thick timber, loosed the tethers of the horses and walked deeper into the black woods. It would be foolish to try to pass this way with obvious watchers. He would need to search for another route and hope he could find the village that he had no idea of its location. A flat shoulder at the bank of a stream not more than two hand-widths wide offered him a camp site for the present. He dropped the saddles from the horses, tethered them close by and dropped to his blankets to consider his predicament. He needed to find another route that would keep him from the creek bottom and that would have to be in the daylight. Although he preferred to travel in the darkness, there were limitations and finding a new trail was one of those limitations.

CHAPTER TWENTY-THREE
SCOUT

IT WAS A SHORT SNOOZE THAT TATUM APPRECIATED, BUT A single shaft of bright sunlight bathed his face and brought him awake. He remembered the Comanche warrior that had waited for him and Tatum grinned at the obvious disappointment of the lone Indian. But now he had to find a different route of travel and since he was somewhat certain of the location of the village, he no longer had to follow the trail left by the captors and their bounty. Foregoing his usual morning coffee, he took his spyglass and walked to a small promontory that overlooked the valley below. Although only a couple hundred yards above the river, it offered a good vantage point. He sat with knees drawn up and, resting his elbows on his knees, he steadied the spyglass and began his scrutiny of the valley.

Across the way, he saw a long rimrock-topped ridge that appeared to follow the valley floor as far as he could see; it reminded him of his mother's apron that had a different colored waistband and apron strings, but held the pleated skirt of the apron. The long ridge bent around the far mountains just like his mother's apron. He turned his glass to survey the valley floor, especially concerned about the warrior from the night before. As he watched, looking at every clump of willows and alders and aspen that followed the river, he thought he would cross over and use the ridge for protection as he continued his search for the village. Satisfied the warrior had followed his band of captors, he rigged the horses and mounted up to cross the valley and maybe find a game trail that would lead him to the village.

The crossing of the valley and the Cucharas River, creek though it was, he now worked his way to the top of the ridge, always watching for a game trail that would parallel the ridge and keep him in sight of the valley floor. The steep hillside proved more challenging than what his visual survey suggested and there were no apparent game trails that suited his purpose. Nearing the rimrock, he looked for a break in the escarpment that would make a crossover possible. He continued his search as he rode along the bottom of the slide rock that had, over time, fallen from the rim above him. After almost a quarter hour of difficult travel with the horses having to pick every step among the jumble of stones, Tatum spotted a slight trail, more of a depression, that showed the passage of animals but nothing recent as the trail was grown over with ground-covering mountain greenery. He dismounted and walked ahead, leading his horses, as he examined the trail and kept looking at the rimrock. A break in the slide rock showed the trail mounted to the rim and just behind a talus that stood as a prominent outcropping, the trail used a break in the rimrock to cross over the top.

Tatum grinned as he mounted up and pointed the sorrel to the trail. With a quick thought, he stopped and surveyed the valley below, wondering if he would be seen as he crossed. But, with no alternative, he gigged his horse forward. As he neared the granite facade, he saw the steep trail between the clifflike sides and knew if he tried to stay aboard, his added weight could easily topple his horse over backwards and kill them both. He took his riata from the saddle and fashioned a halter for his sorrel, lashed the lead rope at its full length to the saddle horn, and started scrambling up the steep trail. Using his hands as much as his feet, he clawed his way to the top of the chute-like trail. He sat down to catch his breath and looked down at his sorrel that had watched him climb before him and now looked at him expectantly.

Tatum scooted to the edge, dug in his heels, and spoke to the sorrel, "Come on, Red, you can do it. If I can, you can," and tugged on the riata. The sorrel dropped his head and took a tentative step, another, and—digging in his front hooves—he arched his back and pushed with his haunches and humped his way to the top, making Tatum roll out of his way. As he reached the crest, the lead rope of the big bay went taut and the packhorse followed the sorrel and scratched his way to the top. Both horses stood with sides heaving and the sorrel bent his neck to look back at Tatum with a look that expected praise; Tatum willingly gave it, walking to the side of the gelding, talking all the way, and rubbed his neck and face as he offered his praise. The bay jealously nudged him with his nose as if asking for his share of praise, and Tatum rubbed the bay's face and neck and praised him as well. Both horses pushed back against his hand and enjoyed the brief interlude.

As Tatum surveyed the narrow ridge, he saw the slope on the side opposite the Cucharas River was an easy grade that sloped to the wide draw that separated the ridge from the taller mountains to the east. He mounted the sorrel and nudged them off the ridge to the tree-covered slope on the east side. Within thirty yards they came to a game trail that appeared to parallel the ridge and Tatum reined the horses to follow the trail. Well protected from sight in the dark timber,

Tatum relaxed and enjoyed the easy gait of the sorrel as he shuffled along the path. A sudden noise from in front and below caused Tatum to rein up and stand in his stirrups to search the timber for the source of the disruption. He smelled them before he saw them; four cow elk and three calves crashed through the timber below. The scattered aspen and thinning pines gave way to the leggy brown creatures that moved, not as spooked but anxious to find their graze for the day.

Tatum grinned as he watched the family of forest creatures go about their daily business and thought about the wide variety of animals in these beautiful mountains and the many members of mankind, both good and evil. He sat back in his saddle and nudged his sorrel forward to continue their quest for the Comanche village. He thought about what he would do when he found it, but knew it was futile to think about something he hadn't seen and had never encountered before. As was his usual practice, he would take it as it comes.

It was approaching mid-day when Tatum noticed the valley to the east of the ridge widening and the tree line edge up the side slope. He reined up and dismounted, ground tying his horses and, with Hawken in hand, walked to the thinning trees for a better view of what lay ahead. To his surprise, he saw a wide grassy flat that held what he considered to be a huge Indian village. He was well back and away, about a half mile from the large cluster of tepees, and he stood beside a tall ponderosa as he looked at the scene below. He returned to the horses, took his spyglass from the saddle bags and walked back to the tall pine. He scanned the many buffalo hide lodges, searching for any sign of the captives and saw none. The village was busy with the usual activities with women preparing meals and children playing while warriors sat and talked, some working with arrows and other accouterments. He looked around to see if he might find a better vantage point and saw the ridge above and behind him now sloped away to a point past the village. Although the tree cover was so sparse as to not provide sufficient cover, there was an escarpment just below the last point of rimrock that would suit his purpose.

He returned to the horses and moved back into the black timber searching for a place that would provide cover and feed for the horses, and protection from any passersby. He soon found a small glade with a nearby spring and de-rigged and picketed the horses. Once his camp was secure, he started off on foot to make his way to the previously seen promontory to search the village for any sign of the women.

CHAPTER TWENTY-FOUR
ENTRY

Tatum lay belly down, slowly moving his spyglass as he scanned the entire village. After watching for about a half hour, he was beginning to wonder if the war party had returned with the captives or killed them on the trail. There had been no sign of the captives being left behind for the first day's travel or even the second day's route. But anything could have happened on the trail after Tatum crossed the valley and no longer followed the captors. He shook his head as he thought about the women and looked again at the village of over eighty lodges. If they were there, they were kept in one of the lodges, but they had to let them out sometime for them to relieve themselves.

Tatum moved back from the edge of the promontory and sat back against a large boulder that marked the end of the rimrock. He considered the problem and thought about the four women and what must be happening with them. They were the last of those stricken with the illness and were still helping with those that had developed the abscesses and couldn't help themselves so they would not have been in the wagons when the attack came and were more vulnerable to capture. But with the two days travel, they would soon develop the abscesses that would be visible to their captors. He calculated he had maybe a day before that happened and then there would be no way of knowing what the Comanche would do once they saw the effects of the disease. He didn't know if any of those in the village knew anything about smallpox, but he could only assume they were ignorant of the disease and its effects.

He bellied down again for another look and had no sooner lifted the spyglass to his eye than he spotted a commotion near one of the lodges toward the center of the village. As he trained the glass, he saw two women fighting over something; it was one of the checkered quilts from the wagons. Now he knew for certain the captors had returned, but he still didn't know about the women. He sat back and considered his options and all he could think of was to ride straight into the camp. He knew many tribes considered their camp as a refuge and anyone that was within the camp would be safe no matter who they were and as long as they did nothing to raise the wrath of the people. But that safety only extended within the camp and, even then, there were no guarantees that this tribe ascribed to that tenet.

He walked back to his horses and resigned himself to what he considered his only option. He mounted up and started for the village. There were no trails that approached the village from this direction, with most of the trails into the village coming from south of the camp. The community was situated in a bit of a bowl with the only source of water coming from behind Tatum and the village herd was grazing in the two offshoot valleys on the east edge of the flat that sloped gently away. He passed the horse herd, still holding near the tree line, and slowly approached the village. His Hawken was in the scabbard and he held both hands palm open and shoulder high, guiding his mount with leg pressure.

He was first spotted by two women that were walking with buffalo-bladder water containers to the small stream and they stopped, frozen in place, as they watched the white man near their village. Soon others saw the man approaching and sounded the alarm causing the usual activity to cease. Even the naked children, accustomed to playing without interruption, stopped and ran to their mothers' sides. Several warriors, a few carrying war shields and lances, others with bows with nocked arrows, walked toward the intruder. He continued toward the center of the camp, looking at those that watched him, and was surprised when he saw an old woman looking up at him who had pockmarks on her face like those that survived smallpox. Much of the crowd followed with no one stopping him but several walking alongside. Most were talking among themselves and gesticulating toward the rider, some of the younger warriors shouting at him. As he neared what appeared to be a central compound with a large fire circle in the middle, one of the warriors grabbed the reins of the sorrel and stopped Tatum. As he looked around, Tatum saw several somber looking warriors, obviously leaders of some sort, standing shoulder to shoulder and looking sternly at this new arrival.

One man stepped forward. He was broad shouldered with very long braids that held a touch of grey and hung almost to his waist; braided with tufts of beaver fur, the part down the center of his skull was painted with bright vermillion. A tattoo of some geometric design marked the side of his face and extended down his neck. A hammered gold band circled his arm at the top of his bicep. He wore fringed buckskin leggings, a beaded breech-cloth, a bone breastplate and a blanket over one shoulder. He was an intimidating figure as he spoke firmly to Tatum in the Comanche tongue. He immediately recognized that Tatum did not understand what he said so he motioned to a woman standing at the edge of the crowd who stepped forward and spoke in English.

"Buffalo Hump asks why you are here," she said without looking at Tatum.

Tatum looked at the translator and said, "Tell Buffalo Hump that I am here for the women that were taken from the wagons by your war party," and looked up at the chief.

When she translated, several people murmured among themselves, but the chief was unmoved. He responded to the translator who turned to Tatum and said, "Buffalo Hump asks why he should let you have these women. He also asks who you are and why are you so stupid to come into the village by yourself," and looked up at the white man, smiling at the remark of her chief.

Tatum smiled back at her and said, "I am known by the Osage as TatumTatum, and the Kiowa call me Long Bow. Carson called me Tate. I heard that Buffalo Hump was a man of honor and would not make war on a few defenseless women and I came in by myself because there was no one else stupid enough to come with me." She grinned at him and turned to translate.

The chief also chuckled at his response and started to speak when he was interrupted by a warrior from behind Tatum that screamed, "Aiiieeeee!" and came forward waving an arrow taken from the quiver tied to the parfleche on the packhorse. As Tatum twisted around in his saddle to see the young warrior waving the arrow overhead and starting to shout in the language of the Comanche, he saw it was one of his arrows and realized this man had recognized it as one like those that had downed two warriors of the band that pursued the wagon train. He hung his head at his stupidity, knowing this could be his undoing and that with that simple mistake, the fat was in the fire.

Tatum was pulled from his saddle by a couple of angered warriors that pummeled him as he fell to the ground. Many were shouting and screaming as the crowd surged forward and around the downed white man, but the shouted command of the chief and the added shouts of those near him stilled the crowd and they moved away from Tatum. The chief and two of the men that stood beside him pushed through the crowd and spoke to the angry mob, some that started to argue back but were stilled by his upraised hand. At his command, two warriors stepped forward and took hold of Tatum's arms, disarmed him and walked him to a nearby tepee, pulled the flap back and pushed him through the opening.

He stumbled into the lodge, falling forward on a blanket that covered the ground and heard the gasps of several around him. He pushed himself up on hands and knees and looked around to see the four women captives. They started talking all at once and Tatum lifted his hands to still them, sat up and looked at them and said, "Hello, ladies, fancy meeting you here."

They couldn't help themselves and grinned at Tatum's greeting and started asking questions. "What are they going to do with us, Tate?" asked Rosa, obviously weak and scared.

He looked at each of the women, thinking about the stage of the disease and saw Rosa and Adriana both had rashes on their face and arms but Caterina and Valentina showed nothing more than weakness and fear.

"I'm not sure but if I can talk to them and explain a few things, maybe we can get out of here. To be honest with you ladies, I'm more concerned about your sickness. I see you and you," nodding to Rosa and Adriana, "already have the rash and by tonight, at the latest in the morning, you'll break out in the blisters. I need to talk to them before that."

"But how? You don't know their language, do you?" asked Rosa.

"No, but there is a woman out there that does; she translated for me."

"Then why did they put you in here?"

"Uh, they recognized the arrows from my pack. See, when I hung back from the wagons, I used my longbow to try to discourage them from following and I killed a couple of their men. Apparently, the one that recognized the arrows was not too happy about it, maybe related to them, so they threw me in here." He shrugged his shoulders as he looked at the women. They sighed and looked away, wondering what would happen next. They were afraid, and rightly so. Carson had told him about the Comanche taking captive women and trading them to the Mexican Comancheros or traders who would take the captives and sell them into bondage south of the border. But first they had to survive and Tatum was thinking long and hard about what next.

He stepped to the entry flap and slowly lifted it to peer out and had his hand slapped by the guard standing directly in front of the flap. He spoke loudly from behind the flap, saying "Get the woman to speak for me!" and again lifted the flap. This time he could open it farther and look at the guard. Using hand signs and speaking aloud as well, he thought he got his message across as the warrior motioned him with nodded head but also signaled for him to shut the flap. Now he had to wait.

CHAPTER TWENTY-FIVE
DIALOGUE

SHE PUSHED THE ENTRY COVER AWAY AND STEPPED INSIDE, standing with her back to the entry and as close to the skin of the tepee as possible. She looked at Tatum as he stood across the fire circle from her and waited for his question. He looked at her and motioned for her to sit and she refused as she asked, "You asked for me to come. What is it you need?"

He looked at her, detecting her distrust and doubt, but began, "I need to talk to Buffalo Hump and explain something to him about these women," motioning around the circle at the seated women. "They are sick, and the sickness they have could pass to many of your people and many could die."

She showed alarm with wide eyes and uplifted eyebrows, then looked around at the women. Tatum walked to Rosa and pointed to the rash on her face and arms, and to Adriana as well. "This will get worse, and many that get this disease will die. But if Buffalo Hump acts soon, maybe we can prevent this spotted disease from affecting so many people."

He noticed her look up at him when he said 'spotted disease' and he asked her, "Do you know of this spotted disease?"

"There is an old woman, Dark Cloud, that has marks on her face and body and she says it is from the spotted disease. It was before my time, and most here do not know of it."

"Can you bring her and me to Buffalo Hump so we can tell him about it?" asked Tatum, somewhat encouraged that there was a survivor in the village that could tell of the disease. Maybe with this woman's story, he could convince Buffalo Hump to take action.

The translator, White Feather, nodded her head and said, "I will get the old woman and come back for you. Then we will speak to Buffalo Hump." She quickly turned and stepped from the tepee, leaving Tatum and the women hopeful of possible help. Within moments, the hide was thrown back and White Feather motioned for Tatum to follow.

As they approached the large lodge that was at the edge of the central compound, a woman was busy at the cook fire and as they neared, she stood and entered the lodge. Shortly, Buffalo Hump exited the lodge followed by another warrior that had the top of the skull of a buffalo complete with horns and hide atop his head as a headdress. The cape of the buffalo trailed down his back and tassels of bright yellow hung at the side. He also carried a club with opposing horns filled with small stones that rattled as he moved. Tatum immediately identified him as a shaman.

Buffalo Hump stood with one hand holding the blanket across his shoulder and looked at White Feather, waiting for her to speak. She looked to Tatum and he began, "Buffalo Hump, the women from the wagons are sick. All the people at those wagons were sick and some were dying, as these women might also." Tatum waited for the woman to translate and watched the reaction of the chief. He continued, "And this disease they have is the spotted disease like your Dark Cloud," motioning to the old woman that stood nearby, "suffered long ago."

As White Feather spoke and motioned to the old woman, Tatum noticed the reaction of alarm that painted the face of the chief. "But if we act soon, we can save many of your people." White Feather translated, and the chief looked at Tatum and asked, "How do we know they are sick with the spotted disease. None of them have those spots," motioning to the lodge with the women.

"Well, Chief, you can wait until tomorrow when the spots start to show and look at them, but you will become sick, too. Or you can take my word for it and we can start to help your people before too many get sick and die."

Buffalo Hump looked to his shaman, Black Bull, and the two conferred for a moment before Buffalo Hump turned back to Tatum. "What is it you would do?" he asked.

Tatum had a sudden thought and said, "First, I would like to talk with your shaman and maybe together we can decide what to do," as he nodded toward Black Bull, conceding his importance in matters of sickness and treatments. The chief nodded to Tatum and to Black Bull, yielding to his shaman and motioning for him to take Tatum to his lodge for this counsel. With a stiff wave of his horn club, the shaman led off and was followed by Tatum and White Feather and Dark Cloud.

The inside of the shaman's lodge was filled with dried plants hanging from above, several parfleches stacked to the side, probably containing his many herbs and plants for healing, and several fetishes hanging near the bundles of plants. Other totems and talisman and carved images could be seen on containers and hanging from looped braids. Tatum gave a cursory glance to the items, accepted the offered seat on a stack of robes and waited for the shaman to give him his attention. Tatum began, "This disease is very deadly and let me explain to you how it spreads and progresses." White Feather diligently translated as Tatum explained and the shaman listened, asked occasional questions, and often showed surprise and alarm as Tatum detailed the toll of the disease. As he spoke, Black Bull looked to Dark Cloud for her response and was repeatedly met with her agreement, shown by her almost continually nodding head. When Tatum paused, Dark Cloud began to tell of her experience from over two decades past.

"I was the age of White Feather," and nodded toward the younger woman, "when the spotted disease came to our village. Almost everyone took ill, but it took time as the white man has said. The children died soon after they started with the spots, but men and women struggled longer. When the color turns on the face and arms, soon the spots will come. Everyone that was near soon became ill. This many," and she showed both hands with all fingers extended meaning the number ten, "died every day and the sickness stayed for more than a moon. Every one of the village but this many," and she held only one hand with all fingers extended, "went to the other side."

White Feather translated the words of the old woman to Tatum, and he dropped his head at the thought of almost three hundred of their people dying to smallpox. He later learned it was in 1817 and was among the Kwaar, a different band from the Yapai led by Buffalo Hump. Tatum looked to Black Bull and said, "So you see, Black Bull, we must go to work right away, and I think we should start by isolating those that have been exposed, either to the women directly or to the things of the women, blankets and such. If we keep them apart and anyone else that begins to show symptoms, I think we can stop it before it goes too far."

After listening to White Feather's translation, Black Bull looked at Tatum and asked, "Why do you do this? You are our enemy."

"No, Black Bull, I am not your enemy. I fought to defend my friends, just like you would. But now, I cannot let this disease destroy your people. What kind of a man would that make me if I could help and did not?"

Black Bull looked intently at Tatum as he spoke and when he fell quiet, Black Bull grunted, stood and motioned for Tatum to follow. The two women also followed, and Tatum turned to White Feather and asked, "Would Dark Cloud be willing to help? Since she has had the pox, she can't get it again and she could be very helpful." White Feather asked the old woman who flashed a rare smile and nodded her head. Tatum saw her reaction and motioned to his heart and hers and expressed his thanks with the sign. She vigorously nodded her head in understanding and White Feather said, "I think she is happy to be of use again. Most of our people only tolerated her because of her scars, but I believe she will be happy to help."

When they returned to the lodge of Buffalo Hump, Black Bull gave a quick explanation and turned and started barking commands to the few that were gathered nearby. Tatum interjected, "Be sure no one else handles the blankets or other items. They can tell us," and pointed to Dark Cloud and himself, "and we will get them. They must be burnt right away, and anything else they have touched." Large eyes from Black Bull showed his concern, but he condescended and barked more orders. Within moments, the entire village was like a beehive full of angry bees as people scurried to do as they were bidden. It was the custom of the people to burn the personal possessions of the deceased so the idea of burning these things of those that might be affected met little resistance. Tatum stood beside Black Bull and watched as a people that were flirting with panic scurried to do what they could to avoid this terrible thing called smallpox.

SMOKE ROSE OVER THE VILLAGE AS THE MORNING SUN SHOWED its face beyond the Spanish Peaks. Although mostly from the items stolen from the wagons, other blankets and possessions of those thought to be contagious found their way to the smoldering pile. The people had removed several tepees to give a wide barrier of about twenty yards between the quarantined and the rest of the village. As Tatum shared the timing and symptoms of the disease with Black Bull, the shaman used the information to his advantage and directed the people as if everything was of his own doing. Tatum wasn't concerned with credit or power, just stopping the spread of smallpox and if Black Bull wanted to use his totems and treatments, he saw no harm coming from the Shaman's actions.

Rosa and Adriana were both showing abscesses and their discomfort had become misery. Nothing could be done to remove their aggravation but to give them water and try to make them as comfortable as possible. It was as much, if not more so, an anxiety of the mind for they knew that few survived and the thought that the end of their life was near was devastating to the young women. Their pleading eyes filled with tears tore at the hearts of their helpers, and Tatum was not immune to their struggle. He sat by them, held their hands and prayed with them, and did his best to encourage them. But little comfort was realized.

Tatum left the lodge and walked the perimeter of the village, considering what had transpired in such a short time. He had come to the mountains to be alone and yet at every turn he was thrust into the midst of people and their problems. Whether with white men or Indians, it was the same, and all he wanted was to be alone. But he couldn't turn his back when he was needed, and he certainly didn't search out those that were in challenging situations. Maybe after this was all over he would go to the high country and totally isolate himself from people, if that were possible. As he strolled, he watched the activity of the camp. Naked children were playing today, just like yesterday and the day before. Their innocence protected them from the concerns of the adults, but Tatum knew that the children would not be immune to the disease and that several would be stricken. He wondered if it was better not to know or to be informed and face the problem. But he knew that it is only with knowledge that people can prepare for life's challenges.

His stroll brought him to the central compound. He wanted to talk with Black Bull and, seeing White Feather, asked if she would accompany him to see the shaman. She agreed and as they approached his lodge, Black Bull stepped out and greeted them. Minus his headdress of the buffalo horns, he was less intimidating but still an imposing figure. Long braids hung over his bare shoulders and a small braid called a scalp lock was decorated with bits of cloth and a single feather. Tatum began to question him. "Uh, Black Bull, I wanted you to know that two of the white women have the spots and might die soon. That made me think about their burial and what is the custom of your people. What would you have me do about burying the women?" He hated the thought of considering their burial even before they died but with the problem increasing daily, he had to be prepared. When White Feather translated, the shaman looked at the white man and asked, "What is your custom?"

"Well, we bury them and out here in the wild, we would usually cover the graves with stones just to keep any animals from digging into the grave. But that's about all. Nothing special, I reckon."

As Black Bull listened, he nodded his head in under-standing and motioned for White Feather to explain their custom. She began, "When one passes to the other side, we wrap their body in blankets and one will take the body to a burial, maybe a cave, place the body and cover it with stones. When he returns, the mourners burn all his possessions. If the dead has a wife or husband, they show their grief by slashing," and motioned as if cutting her arm with a knife, "their arms."

"I see," replied Tatum. "Is there a cave nearby that we can use, and can we put more than one in the same cave?"

Black Bull anticipated his question and said, "There is a place, *Po-a-cat-le-pi-le-carre*, medicine rock, and there is a large cavern that could be used."

"When the time comes, I will need someone to show me the way. If there are others, I will take them to the cave so no one else is infected," stated Tatum.

"I will show the way; there are things I must do when they are put under the stones," explained Black Bull through the translator. Tatum nodded his head in understanding and excused himself to return to the lodge of the women. One of the Comanche women had been given the task of preparing food for the captives and was busy at the cook fire in front of the lodge. Tatum didn't want to see her infected and he motioned for her to not enter, but to scratch on the lodge and he would come out. As he entered the tepee, the added light from the entry splashed on the women and Tatum saw the sisters, Caterina and Valentina, had developed the rash and it had spread down their arms. They looked up as he entered, sad eyes telling him they knew of their fate.

Tatum's weapons had been returned to him, but he carried only the knife in its sheath at his back and the tomahawk tucked in his belt at his side. He saw no reason to carry the Colt or Hawken, and his longbow and quiver of arrows lay beside them near the outer wall of the lodge. He had a pallet of blankets and a buffalo robe for his bed and his portion of the lodge with the women captives and he sat on the blankets. He looked around at the women, asked the sisters about Rosa and Adriana that were sleeping, and one of the girls replied, "No better, but it is good they are resting. They say the blisters are very painful and it is hard to sleep, but they have been asleep for a while. I'm sure they'll wake soon."

She had no sooner said they would wake when Rosa moaned and rolled to her side, opening her eyes to the others. She looked at Tatum and tried to smile as she started to speak, but her words were hard coming and difficult to hear. Tatum went closer to her side and took her hand, listening. She spoke softly as she said, "My momma said you were a saint, and you are. Thank you for what you've done; it means a lot to us. I know I will soon be with my family. I know that because I said the prayer you told us about. Thank you." She closed her eyes and lay back on the bundle of blankets that served as her pillow. Tatum stood and walked from the lodge into the afternoon glare of bright sunlight and used his neckerchief to wipe the tears from his eyes.

"Aaiiiiieeeee!" came the scream from behind the lodge and Tatum turned quickly to face the charging warrior that held a lance at his side and hate in his eyes. It was the same warrior that had plucked an arrow from Tatum's quiver and had the white man taken as a captive. But now Tatum was armed although he didn't want to break the tradition of the people and do something that would endanger the others. But he couldn't just stand and let the crazed Comanche run him through. Tatum snatched the tomahawk from his belt and dropped into a crouch as the warrior charged. As he neared, he thrust with the lance and Tatum knocked the point aside with his tomahawk and spun away from the Indian and let him pass. The warrior turned around and swung the lance again, seeking to impale Tatum, narrowly missing his side but catching a bit of his buckskin shirt with the tip and tearing it. Tatum staggered aside, but kept his balance as the screaming warrior lifted the lance as if to throw it. Tatum shifted side to side, wary of a throw, and watching the eyes of the warrior. Another scream and he charged with the lance overhead and holding it with both hands. Tatum staggered back and fell, but as the lance came down he rolled aside, striking at the warrior's legs with his tomahawk and connecting. The Indian stumbled and fell to the side and Tatum, seeing his opening, lunged to the fallen man, straddled him and raised his tomahawk ready to split his skull. He brought the hawk down to the side of the warrior's head and cut off a length of his braid.

Tatum stood and looked down at the attacker as he slipped his tomahawk behind his belt at his waist, turned and walked away. A crowd had gathered after the first scream of the attacker and now parted to let Tatum pass. A low murmur passed through the crowd and Tatum saw Buffalo Hump walking to the crowd to see what had happened.

As Tatum walked to the lodge, the woman was still tending the stew pot hanging over the fire and he sat on a stone to collect his thoughts. He wondered if the attacker was a relative or friend of one of the warriors he dropped with his warning arrows to the Comanche pursuing the wagons. That was the only explanation he could find for the man's attack. But he was certain Buffalo Hump would be talking to him about it soon. He would just have to wait and deal with it as it came like he always did. Good or bad, it was beyond his control.

CHAPTER TWENTY-SEVEN
TENDING

BOTH PASSED IN THE NIGHT. TATUM, USUALLY A LIGHT SLEEPER, heard nothing. Their ragged breathing and muted moans had become a part of the night sounds but when they stopped, he had not stirred. He rose from his blankets and knew something was different; the smell of death filled the lodge and he looked at the still forms of Rosa and Adriana and knew. The blankets did not move with their breathing and eyes open as slits showed no life. He quietly moved to their sides and gently pulled the blankets to cover their heads. He didn't want to disturb the sisters and silently moved the entry cover aside and stepped from the tepee.

The village was quiet as the first light of morning pushed its way above the mountains, chasing clouds of soft pinks. Tatum saw a few women rekindling their cooking fires—fires that in the cold months would be inside the tepees—to start the day's routine. He would need his packhorse and he would have to tell Black Bull, but he went to the untended coals in the fire circle by their lodge and added some sticks to start the fire. He needed some coffee and went to the packs stacked beside the lodge, secured his coffee pot and a bag of Arbuckle's to return to the fire. He poured water from the bladder by the stones and set the pot at the edge of the fire. It would take a few moments to catch the bay and bring him back to the lodge.

When he returned, the sisters sat side by side on the grey log, staring at the fire. They looked up as Tatum returned and dropped their heads to retreat back into the mindlessness of the fire. He added Arbuckle's to the water and sat down beside the girls. He spoke softly, "Ladies, I will go inside and take care of Rosa and Adriana. It's really quite simple. I'll just wrap them in blankets and then, if you'd like, we can share a few moments, maybe have a prayer. Afterwards, I'll take them for burial. It's too far for you to go and it would serve no purpose. There's a cavern in a place called Medicine Rock where they will be buried."

Both girls just nodded their heads in understanding and turned back to the flames. He knew their thoughts were about themselves rather than the friends that passed and he understood. There was nothing he could say that would change anything. He stepped to the fire to pick up the pot and poured a cup of coffee. He remained standing and found himself staring at the fire and thinking about the loss of the two women and the probable loss of those that sat before him. How quickly life can be taken and how few the days that are shared. Thinking of his own parents, he realized afresh the value and the brevity of moments with loved ones.

He tossed the dregs of his coffee, sat down his cup and walked away to complete his duty of telling Black Bull of the passing of the women. Using crude sign language and a few words of Comanche he had grasped, he got the message across and understood Black Bull to say he would be ready for the trek to the burial site. With a heavy sigh, he returned to the lodge and entered to prepare the ladies for their last journey.

When he finished, he stuck his head out of the tepee, motioned to the sisters and held the entry cover aside for them to enter. Both bodies were wrapped in blankets and had a rawhide thong wrapped around the blankets to secure the covering. When the girls looked at the bundles, they both put their hands to their mouths, turned to one another and sobbed on each other's shoulders. Tatum waited for them to be ready and when they separated from one another, they looked at him and nodded. He reached out to take their hands and bowed his head as he started to pray, "Lord, we're hurting today. Our friends have passed and left us with tears and sadness, but we are thankful to know they are with you today. And that they are with their families as well. Maybe they're having a family reunion and happy to be together. Lord, you said in your Psalms that, because they loved you, you would set them on high and for that we thank you Lord. Now, we also ask that you take care of these two sisters 'cuz you said in that same Psalm that you would deliver them from the pestilence, and we're asking for that." Tatum looked at the girls and bowed his head again. "And that's all, I guess. Amen."

At the 'Amen' the girls lifted their heads to Tatum and smiled and Caterina said, "Thank you, Tate, thank you."

"Well, you girls just take it easy today, get some rest and I'll be back in a while. I don't know 'zackly how soon 'cuz I ain't never been there, but I don't think it'll be too long." They nodded their understanding and moved to their blankets to give him room to take the bundles from the tepee. Black Bull was waiting by the cook fire when Tatum exited the lodge with the first bundle and stood back to watch him lay the body on the packhorse. He started a low chant, occasionally shaking his horned club that rattled, made a few slow steps side to side, and waited for Tatum to secure the second body. When Tatum nodded to Black Bull, the shaman started away from the lodge and led him from the village as several people stood respectfully by and watched.

Medicine Rock was about four miles from the village and the trail was easy until they neared the mountain. The rocky hillside was marked by a prominent pillar of stone, sided by three others, and many large boulders were strewn across the face of the somewhat steep hillside. Twisted cedar and stunted pinion found little purchase in the limited soil but cacti, both cholla and prickly pear, grew in abundance. They followed a switchback trail to the hidden entrance of the large cavern and Black Bull produced two torches previously hidden behind a nearby boulder. The heads of the torches were thickly daubed with pine pitch and Black Bear motioned for Tatum to start a flame to ignite the torches. He ground tied the bay at the entrance to the cavern, withdrew a flint and steel from his possibles pouch and with some tinder and twigs from the cedar, he soon had a small flame sufficient to ignite the torches.

Black Bull led the way into the cavern that surprised Tatum with the size of the first huge chamber. Formations of stalagmites and stalactites danced in the shadows from the torches and Tatum stopped to look at the impressive figures in stone. Black Bull grunted at his pause and with a wave of the torch bid Tatum to follow. A smaller chamber opened from the entry hollow and at Black Bull's motioning, Tatum knew this was where the bodies were to be placed. He untied the rawhide holding the bodies in place and as gently as possible lay them side by side near the back wall of the dark room. At the side of the chamber were several stones, apparently from a partial cave-in, and Tatum quickly covered the two bodies.

While Tatum worked, Black Bull chanted and ignited some type of dried plant that emitted a pleasing aroma with its smoke as the shaman waved it back and forth. Tatum did not know the purpose, maybe to dispel spirits or just to allay the smell of death, but he did not interfere with the shaman's work. Tatum took a last look at the burials, nodded his head and thought to himself, *Good bye Rosa, good bye Adriana,* and turned to leave, leading the bay from the chambers and was followed by Black Bull. When they exited the cavern, Tatum paused and turned to Black Bull and said, "Thank you, Black Bull, thank you." The shaman nodded his head in understanding and the two men started their return to the village.

As they walked side by side, there seemed to be an understanding between them. Even though the barrier of language separated them, the bond of companions in difficult times brought them closer. They both knew they would be making this trip all too often in the days to come. Tatum determined the next trip, he would be riding the sorrel instead of shank's mare.

It was mid-day when they returned to the village and Tatum went straight to the lodge to check on the sisters. The Comanche woman was tending the cook fire and had something going in the cookpot, but the sisters were not outside. When Tatum stepped inside, he saw the girls were in their blankets and dozing, but they stirred when he entered. Caterina raised her arm and motioned him near. He stepped to her side and knelt beside her and took her outstretched hand. She looked at him and motioned with her free hand toward some abscesses at her jaw and on her neck. Tatum nodded his head, sorrow filling his eyes, and started to speak but was stopped with her upraised hand. In a soft voice she said, "My sister and I are determined to fight this. We don't want to go as the others did, we are going to fight. Please stay with us," and her eyes spoke more clearly than her voice. He replied, "I will be right here with you. You will not be alone." She formed the words with her lips, but her voice was too low to hear as she said, "Thank you." She turned her head to the skin of the tepee and closed her eyes, squeezed his hand and let go. Tatum watched her for a moment and reassured by her steady breathing, stood to go to the fire and get something to eat. He was pleased with her fighting spirit and thought, *That's the way it should be, fighting tooth and nail all the way. Don't give up, ever!*

CHAPTER TWENTY-EIGHT
DUTY

TATUM'S MUSING WAS INTERRUPTED WHEN HE HEARD approaching footfalls and looked up to see the approach of Buffalo Hump and Black Bull and two others approaching. He watched with a somber face and waited for them to start the dialogue. White Feather came from the side, apparently previously bidden, and stopped well back from the leaders and dropped her head to await her summons. Buffalo Hump began and paused for White Feather to interpret.

"Our chief has come to explain about White Horse, the one who attacked you."

Tatum nodded and looked to Buffalo Hump, waiting.

"White Horse was grieved when your arrow killed his brother. But what he did was against our custom; a visitor within our village is to be treated as one of us. When you cut his braid, it was a shame to him. He has been banished from our people."

"Uh, Chief, I understand his grief. I thought that was why he attacked, and that is why I chose not to kill him. Can he return to his people?" asked Tatum as he motioned to the village with a sweep of his arm.

"No, his shame is now our shame. You have been a help by warning us of the sickness. And as you said, several of our people have now become ill. But after this passes, and if you leave us, White Horse will still want his vengeance."

This was the first word that Tatum had received that some of the villagers had been stricken with the first stages of the disease and he shook his head at the news.

"I wish I had been wrong, Buffalo Hump, but now we must be careful with the others." Tatum looked at Black Bull and said, "We must make sure that anyone that is not in the lodges of the sick but comes down with the sickness, that they are quickly brought to the others and we must try to keep it from spreading."

Black Bull nodded and added, "I have used my smoke and my prayers, but I have also told the people to bring any others to us immediately."

"Well, Black Bull, we need your prayers and anything else you can do. Perhaps you will be able to make this less than what I fear. I hope so," replied Tatum and looked back to Buffalo Hump. "I'm sorry about White Horse, but right now my concern is for the rest of the people. The other two women have shown the spots so I dunno what's next."

Buffalo Hump, Black Bull, and the others left Tatum standing by his fire and he was surprised that White Feather remained behind. She looked at the white man that was helping her people and smiled as she said, "I want to help you."

Tatum was pleased with her desire to help but he was also concerned. "White Feather, it is good that you want to help, but I don't want you to get any closer than you already have. You could very easily get the disease and I don't want that."

"No, you don't understand. I want to help you learn the language of our people so you can talk to those that are sick and more. I think if you know our language and our customs, you will be able to help more."

He let a slight grin cross his face and said, "You're right. That would make it much easier to do what needs to be done. Alright, let's get started. What should we do?"

"Walk with me," she directed and turned slightly as if to leave. Tatum followed, and they began a walk through the village and she started her instruction by pointing out objects or activities and giving the names, having him repeat them, and on to another. Her coaching included repeatedly sighting the same object or activity and pointing it out and asking him to recall each one. He was surprised how quickly he was learning, and was pleased with White Feather's skill and understanding. The Comanche language was a distinct dialect of the Shoshonean language as the Comanche had broken away from the Shoshone over a hundred years previously. Tatum was eager to learn and continually practiced his rapidly expanding vocabulary. He had learned some Osage when he lived near the Tallchief family, but this was distinctly different and somewhat more challenging.

Twilight quickly settled over the camp and Tatum returned to the lodge with the sisters and White Feather said she would return and continue their lessons on the morrow. When Tatum entered the lodge, the girls were resting but had been talking and encouraging one another and were glad to see Tatum. He brought them bowls of stew which they picked at, ate a little and pushed the bowls aside. Tatum said, "Now ladies, you said you were goin' to fight this thing, and you need strength to do that, so try to eat as much as you can."

Caterina, the more talkative of the two, said, "It's the discomfort that is the worst, Tatum. No matter how we lay, it hurts. We've got sores everywhere!"

"I'm sorry, Cat, but stay with it. I know it's frustrating, I've seen it before. But there's nothing that can be done but for you to fight it." He faced both of the young women with as sober an expression as he could muster. He didn't want to scold them, and he didn't want them to see his dismay. He wanted to hold them and tell them it would be alright, but that would only make it more painful for them. And he couldn't lie to them; he didn't know if it would be alright for very few survived this horrible disease.

He reached out and took one of the girl's hands in each of his and reassured them he would stay near as much as he could. "And I'm still praying for you both and I will keep on prayin' and you need to keep fightin'. Can you do that?"

Both girls nodded and tried to smile before laying their heads back on the bundles for pillows and closing their eyes. Tatum took the bowls and walked from the lodge to get his own portion for supper before turning in for the night. He stuck his head back in the lodge and told the girls to rest easy and that he was going to make a quick check on the others that were showing signs of the sickness. They mumbled their okays and Tatum turned to leave.

There were ten lodges, plus the lodge of the girls, that had been set aside for those that had been exposed. Some held complete families as the warrior had brought blankets and other plunder from the wagons and the family had shared his bounty and now shared the exposure of the disease. Tatum went from lodge to lodge, looking and sometimes examining the different suspicious and scared members of the village. With his limited vocabulary, with the words that Tatum especially sought, he was able to communicate enough to check on the symptoms. There were four warriors, one woman, and two children that were showing the first stages of the disease: fever, vomiting and pain. As he left the collective of the contagious, he thought the disease was spreading more rapidly than usual, but he wasn't certain about anything about this disease; his knowledge was limited.

When he returned to the lodge, the girls were resting although not in a deep sleep; the discomfort kept them semi-awake. He rolled out his bedroll on the far side of the lodge and as he started to stretch out, a moan form Valentina stopped him. He went to her side and she motioned for a drink. He retrieved the gourd from the nearby water container and lifted her head to help her drink. He felt the back of her neck and knew she had a fever. As he lay her back down, he pulled the water bladder closer, dipped a cloth in the water and applied it to the girl's forehead. The sigh emitted by Valentina told of her relief and Tatum repeated the action for Caterina. Both girls were considerably relieved by the cool cloth, and Tatum was beginning to feel more like a mother than a friend. He grinned and shook his head at the thought, but knowing he had given the girls some relief was pleasing to him. He sat by their sides through the night, changing the cloths often, and took a short leave to get fresh water for drinking, and continued his ministrations. He knew the girls felt better and he felt the better for it.

He thought he had just nodded off when he looked up to see the light of day above the smoke flaps and heard a scratching at the entry.

"Long Bow? Are you ready for your lesson?" asked White Feather.

"Uh, sure, sure. I'll be right out," he declared, surprised he had slept even for a short while. He looked to the girls; they were stirring, and he put a fresh cool cloth to each forehead and whispered, "I'm going to be right outside with White Feather. She's teaching me their language. I'll bring you in something to eat as soon as it's ready." Valentina nodded her understanding and tried to smile as she watched him step through the tepee entry.

White Feather had been speaking with the woman that had been given the cooking duty and looked up as Tatum exited the lodge. She smiled and asked if he wanted to walk again. "No, I think I need to stay near the ladies. They're struggling with the worst part, and I'd like to be nearby. But if it's alright with you, I would like you to stick around and continue the lesson."

"Stick around?" she asked, not understanding.

He chuckled and explained, and motioned for her to start her instruction.

CHAPTER TWENTY-NINE
SPREAD

TATUM WALKED BACK FROM THE QUARANTINED COMPLEX shaking his head at how fast the smallpox was spreading among the people. Just three days ago he counted four warriors, one woman, and two children that had the rash. Now, all of those had broken out in the pox and a dozen more had started with the rash and others showed the earlier symptoms. He was thankful there were no reports of others that were not quarantined had fallen ill, but everyone was being very careful. Some of the people had moved their lodges away from the village and formed a small camp a few miles farther away, afraid that even distance could not stop the spread. Tatum couldn't blame them for their fear although none of the Comanche had died yet. But he knew that would soon change. Just the wailing and chanting that came from the lodges was disconcerting but if the others saw the pox, it would be more frightening.

Black Bull and Dark Cloud worked at their tasks tirelessly. Although Black Bull would not get within arm's reach of the afflicted, Dark Cloud didn't hesitate and gave comfort wherever and whenever she could. Tatum tended to many of them, but the mission was more than he could handle by himself and he was rapidly tiring. He breathed deeply as he approached the lodge of the sisters, nodded at the woman at the fire, and pushed the hide that covered the entry aside and stepped into the lodge. With little light coming from the smoke flaps and from below the hide covers behind the lining, what light was there was dim but adequate. Tatum looked first to Caterina, saw she was resting, and looked to Valentina to see her looking directly at him. She tried to force a smile, but was too weak. With her hand held at her chest, she moved her fingers to ask for a drink. Tatum complied and lifted her head to help her drink from the gourd. Pox covered every exposed part of her body and caused her features to be deformed. Those near her eyes made her appear as if she had been in a fight and had her eyes blackened and swollen. With every look, Tatum felt for the young woman but tried to keep a calm demeanor and even a smile. As he looked, he noticed a few of the scabs had dried and some had fallen off and he looked back to see Valentina watching him visually examine her. As he looked in her eyes he saw wonder and fear and forced himself to smile as he said, "When the scabs dry and start to fall off, that's a good sign." He didn't want to say more because he had also seen the same thing with Rosa and Adriana before they died but, at this stage, they were weaker and seemed to have given up. But the sisters were both fighting as they said they would. "I'll get you something to eat," he said as he stood to leave the lodge. She stretched out her arm to stop him and asked, "Do you think . . . " but he held up his hand and said, "Let's hope and pray, and keep fighting."

When he exited the lodge, Black Bull was waiting for him with a dark face and Tatum knew without him saying that someone had died. When he looked at him and waited, Black Bull said, "A child," and hung his head. Tatum was moved by this, the first expression of emotion shown by the shaman; the usually stoic expression required of his duties was momentarily replaced with sadness. Tatum thought the shaman might even be thinking failure, but he knew there was nothing any shaman, for that matter any white doctor, could do to heal someone of this dreaded pestilence. White Feather stepped forward and Tatum told her, "I will come just as soon as I can. I must tend to these two and then I'll come to tend to the child."

Black Bull nodded his acceptance and walked toward his own lodge.

Tatum rode alone with the small bundle strapped behind the cantle of his saddle. It was a familiar trail and he knew it would become even more so in the days ahead. As he neared the cavern, he thought of those that were already there, and remembered the smile and wave of Rosa. He had taken a shine to her, but it was not to be, and soon even the burial crypt would become crowded with others whose lives were cut short. He glanced back at the bundle behind him and remembered the bashful face of the girl that lay on her blankets and looked at him with sorrowful eyes and tears running down her cheeks finding a path of escape between the abscesses. His heavy sigh came as the sorrel stopped at the entrance to the cavern. Tatum stepped down, ground tied the horse and removed the bundle to do his deed.

The news of the first death wasn't taken well by the rest of the villagers and when Tatum returned, he noticed there were more lodges missing, apparently to move to the growing camp farther away. His only concern was that if there was someone infected that had not been found, the disease could spread even further. He turned the sorrel loose with the herd and walked back to the lodge of the sisters and entered. He was surprised to see Valentina sitting up and both girls talking. Caterina had propped her head up so she could see better and talk with her sister and both girls greeted Tatum when he stepped inside.

He responded, "Well, look at you two! Uh, I don't think you should be rushing things just yet, do you?"

Although they spoke just above a whisper, their eyes showed hope and Caterina said, "Oh, we still hurt, but we're trying to ignore it, hoping it'll go away soon."

"I like your spirit!" said Tatum, "Are you ready for something to eat?"

They looked at one another and with a slight nod, gave Tatum the excuse to fetch some food. The same stew simmered in the pot and he dished some into the bowls and returned to the lodge, giving each girl a bowl and carved-bone spoon. He watched as they forced themselves to eat some of the stew, but they soon sat the bowls aside and looked at their angel in buckskins and smiled. This was the first time Tatum felt genuine hope for the girls. He smiled at them and said, "Well, you're still gonna have to get your rest 'cuz I'm thinkin' you're gonna need to be helpin' me 'soons you get better. So, quit lollygaggin' and get well." His hope and spirit were as contagious as the disease had been, and they scooted down into their blankets and lay their heads down to rest. Tatum stepped from the lodge with one last look over his shoulder at the girls.

White Feather was waiting for him by the fire and started right off with her teaching while Tatum took care of the bowls the girls handled. He rinsed them out and set them aside so the woman that cooked wouldn't touch them, and turned his attention fully to White Feather. As she talked, he thought about how attractive she was and wondered about her family. There had been no discussions about each other and all conversation had been strictly concerning the language and names of things, but not about her. As he let his thoughts wander, she looked at him in a quizzical manner and he realized she must have asked him a question. He looked toward her and said, "What?"

"I said, what is the word for hair?"

"Oh, uh, paapi."

"And the word for eyes?"

"Pui. Do you have a husband?" asked Tatum.

White Feather repeated what he said in Comanche, thinking he was asking for the translation of the phrase. But Tatum shook his head, grinning, and asked again, "No, I'm asking you," and pointed at her, "if you have a husband."

She laughed at him and shook her head and said, "No, I do not have a husband. My husband was killed on a raid against the Cheyenne. It is not our custom to talk about those who have crossed over."

"I understand. Do you have any children?"

"No, I have no children. I live in the lodge of my parents. My father is Buffalo Hump."

Tatum nodded his head in understanding as he considered what she said, then asked, "How did you learn to speak English so well?"

"There was a black robe that visited our village when I was younger, and he taught several children about English and the God of your people. Now, what is the word for horse?"

"Puuku."

They continued the lesson in the language of the people until Black Bull came to summon him to the compound of the ill. Tatum looked in on all the lodges and was encouraged to see Dark Cloud doing an excellent job of tending to the needs of the many that were now in different stages of the disease. Only two more showed signs of the illness, but a few of those that took ill early were showing abscesses. Why the disease was progressing so fast bothered Tatum, but he knew his knowledge was limited and accepted the occurrences as they came. There was little else he could do but watch, tend, and wait. He knew some of these might not make it through the night, and more would be down soon.

It was evening when he returned to the lodge of the sisters and he dutifully filled their bowls and carried them in with him as he entered the lodge. Valentina was sitting up again, and he caught her picking at her scabs which he had cautioned her not to do and she dropped her hand immediately like a school girl caught doing something wrong. He chuckled at her response and looked to Caterina to see her dozing but seemingly resting peacefully. He motioned to the bowls and Valentina nodded her head and reached out a hand. He watched as she scooped the stew to her mouth and was pleased that she was eating. It was good to see something good to smile about after leaving so much sadness and fear behind in the camp. Caterina stirred and looked at Tatum, but she wasn't showing the strength of her sister so Tatum helped her and spooned some of the stew for her to eat. She struggled, but showed the same determination as her sister, and downed more than usual. But the doing of it taxed her strength and she begged to lie down.

He watched as she whispered, "Thank you," and closed her eyes. Tatum looked to Valentina and the girl said softly, "Caterina seems to be a little weaker, but she is more of a fighter than I am. I'm sure she'll make it."

Tatum looked from one sister to the other and nodded his head. "Well, let's hope for a restful night for both of you. My ma used to always say, *things always look better in the mornin'*, so we'll just pray for that.

CHAPTER THIRTY
HOPE

FOR FIVE DAYS, TATUM HAD BEEN MAKING THE TREK TO THE
burial crypt. After the first child, each day there were more.
Already today, he had taken the trip with four bundles, and
he was certain he would have to make the trip yet again
before the day was over. He was relieved that no more had
developed the rash or abscesses and he was hopeful none
would. Although there were still several that were suffering
with the pox, most of those were adults. It was the burial of
the children that was the most difficult, once smiling faces
and happy playmates had become small bundles of fear and
death. Each trip grew more difficult and he had quit asking
questions of God. He knew he would never understand but
he remembered his mother saying, "God's ways are not our
ways, and we should be thankful for that." He thought of his
father always trying to teach him at every opportunity but
when Tatum asked his father a question that he couldn't
answer, he would say, "It's always hardest to trust in the dark,
but it's in the dark that faith is strengthened. When we don't
understand, we trust."

When he walked back to the lodge, he was again shown the benefit of that trust when Valentina stepped from the tepee and smiled as he approached. Her sores and scabs had all but disappeared, leaving the white scars common to the survivors of smallpox. But her spirit was undaunted as she stepped to the fire ring and poured Tatum a cup of coffee, and handed it to the tired young man as he took his usual seat on the smooth grey log. As he sipped the warm java, he heard the rustle of the entry cover and looked to see Caterina come from the lodge. She saw Tatum and asked, "Did you leave any of that coffee for the rest of us?"

He looked askance to Valentina and she nodded and motioned to the pot. Caterina poured herself a cup and sat beside Tatum and asked, "How many?"

"Four, so far. But I'll probably have to make another trip later."

"When Val and I went to help, we didn't see any new cases. You think it's stopped?"

"I hope so, but only time will tell." He looked to both of the ladies and said, "You two have been a big help yesterday and today. What with Black Bull down, I'm not sure about the new shaman. Maybe he'll be alright, but he comes across as less trusting than Black Bull."

"I don't understand how that works. Was he Bull's helper or something?" asked Caterina.

"I think it's kinda like an apprentice, you know, like back east in the big city. Printers, wheelwrights, etc., they all have apprentices to learn the trade. I think it's the same way with the shaman. He has to learn all about the plants and herbs and chants and stuff. They actually do a lot of good; many of those plants can be really helpful with different things. They've been usin' 'em for generations and can be mighty good," explained Tatum, thinking about the different plants his friends Red Calf and his father Tall Chief of the Osage had shown him.

As they talked, Tatum watched the approach of the new shaman, Spirit Talker, and his helper. Spirit Talker had assumed the role from Black Bull when the elder had come down with the rash of the pox. The valiant old healer has struggled through the first stages of the disease and kept it from everyone as he carried out his duties, but when the rash came, he knew he could hide it no longer and took his place with the others that were ill. Spirit Talker had studied with Black Bull for over three years; he also knew there was much more for him to learn, but chose bluster and bravado as his tools to hide his lack of knowledge. His helper, Badger, followed close behind, carrying a hollowed horn with a smoldering incense that left a wispy trail of smoke behind.

When he neared the fire circle he stood before but well back from Tatum with arms across his chest and said, "There are two more that must go to the burial cavern, and we will go with you. You did wrong when you took the others without a shaman for the proper burial." It wasn't a question, just an accusatory statement and Tatum's wrinkled brow when he looked at the man showed his concern.

"Black Bull told me to do as I did. You can finish your routine or ceremony for the others when we go there this time," responded Tatum defensively.

"I am the shaman! You will not go near the burial place without me or you will be put to death!" declared Spirit Walker and turned away and walked off without giving Tatum an opportunity to respond. The conversation was possible because of the new shaman's knowledge of English. Before this exchange, Tatum thought the only member of the village that could speak English fluently was White Feather, but Spirit Talker had always been one of the many in the background that had been silent until he was suddenly put in the new role of shaman.

Tatum looked at the sisters and said, "Humm, that's interesting. I think I'm goin' to have to have a talk with Buffalo Hump. In the meantime, maybe you ladies better stay around the lodge and out of Spirit Talker's way. I'm thinkin' he might be wantin' to make trouble for us."

As he walked to the lodge of Buffalo Hump, Tatum thought about the new shaman. As he reflected on the previous days since Black Bull had taken ill, he realized that Spirit Talker had never come near the lodges of those that were down with the pox. His helper, Badger, had been seen in the compound of the afflicted, but never Spirit Talker. And even when he came to Tatum's lodge, he had never entered, although invited, and had always kept his distance from him. As Tatum considered the actions of the new shaman, he knew it was more than just being cautious; he was afraid of the disease. Rightly so, thought Tatum, but that fear was also goading the man to strange behavior and that might cause problems for Tatum and the sisters.

He was greeted by Buffalo Hump from his place of rest against the willow back rest to the side of the lodge entry. He had been working on an arrow shaft when he saw Tatum approach and motioned for the young man to have a seat. Tatum squatted cross-legged as he greeted the chief. White Feather sat beside her father and translated as the conversation began. When Tatum explained his concern regarding Spirit Talker, the chief nodded his head in understanding and when Tatum paused, the chief looked to the man who had helped his people and began to explain.

"Spirit Talker has also come to me and told me his concern. He believes you were responsible for Black Bull getting the spotted disease and he thinks you could cast a spell on him also." Tatum started to interrupt but was stopped by the uplifted hand of the chief as he continued. "I do not believe that to be true. You have helped our people and because you came to warn us, you kept the spotted disease from spreading. For that, I am grateful. Spirit Talker is finding his place as a shaman of the people and he must show he has power. If he can show he has more power than you and the spotted disease, he will make his place among the people. Tell me, Long Bow, has the spread of the spotted disease been stopped?"

"I think so, Chief, but the only way we'll know for sure is with time," answered Tatum.

"Is there anything else you can do but bury the dead?" asked Buffalo Hump

"No, just keep others from handling the dead or sick or whatever they touch."

"Dark Cloud, the old woman has been helping you, has she not?"

"Yes, she has been a big help."

"And she cannot get the disease, but anyone else can, is that right?" asked Buffalo Hump.

"That is right," answered Tatum, wondering where the chief was going with this line of questioning.

"What else must be done?"

"Well, anything and everything that has been touched by those that had the disease must be burned. And, just to be safe, I'd say you need to move your camp well away from here and not return," explained Tatum.

The old chief nodded in understanding and sat quietly for a moment before speaking again. "If you were to leave, Spirit Talker would think his power was greater and if the disease stops, he will take credit for it and his place will be set."

Tatum understood what he was saying and asked, "What about the two white women that survived the pox. Can I take them with me?"

"That would be good. The only reminder we will have of this spotted disease will be the old woman, but she was with us before. Yes, you can take them. I will have horses brought to your lodge as soon as it is dark."

Tatum smiled at the thought of leaving, but knew there was still another trip to take to the burial crypt, and he knew that Spirit Talker would not handle the bodies, leaving the task to Tatum. If he could just get through this trip without any confrontation with the new shaman, then he and the girls could put this entire thing behind them. He stood to leave and reached down to Buffalo Hump and the two clasped forearms and nodded their agreement and appreciation of one another.

Tatum returned to his lodge where he had tethered his horses in anticipation of another trip to the cavern. The sisters were inside the tepee and he stepped in and shared with them the news that they might soon be leaving. The girls were excited about leaving, having often wondered if they would die here and after getting better, wondering if they would still be considered as captives and must spend the rest of their lives with the Comanche. They had not dared to think of their future, but suddenly their minds were flooded with questions and thoughts of possibilities. Looking at one another, they began to chatter like children and then saw Tatum grinning at them and Caterina said, "Well, we didn't know if we would ever be able to leave and now that you say we are, we don't know what to do."

"Well, there's not much for you to do. You shouldn't be taking anything but your clothes and I might even be able to do something about that. But, we haven't left yet, so don't let on to anyone what's goin' on, understand?" Both girls nodded enthusiastically and watched as Tatum stood and explained, "I've got one more trip to make to the burial cavern then I'll be back. So, just fix us somethin' to eat and we'll talk about it more later."

Spirit Talker and Badger followed well behind Tatum and his burdens. With two bundles on the packhorse and one behind the cantle of his saddle, Tatum thought about the only two pox-stricken patients that remained alive, Black Bull and a woman. The woman had continued to fight, not unlike Caterina and Valentina, and might even survive. He would speak to Dark Cloud to make sure she gave the woman extra care. The horses, so familiar with the trail, had brought Tatum to the burial cavern while he had let his mind wander over the recent events and what might be soon coming. The sudden stop brought him from his ponderings and he looked behind him to see the shaman and his helper had also stopped. Tatum stepped down and carried the bundles into the cavern to lay them beside the others. As he placed the last one alongside the others, he stood and counted. Including Rosa and Adriana, there were twenty-one. He finished carrying the stones to place on the recent additions, all the while listening to the drone of the chants of the shaman from the entrance of the cavern. As he stood and stretched, he looked at the wall and roof of the archway to this branch of the cavern and knew it was time.

He had placed one torch near the entry to this room of the cavern and the other further inside to aid in his work. Now, he took both torches, standing one in a crack of stalagmite and using the other, now with the flame out, to wedge behind the rocks at the wall, loosening several and finally causing the roof to start to collapse. He grabbed the other torch and ran from the cavern as the roof of the branch tunnel caved in, sealing off the burial crypt. The dust cloud followed him, and the sudden eruption of noise and dust startled the shaman and his helper; they froze in their dance and chanting as Tatum ran from the entry. He stopped next to his horses that had stepped back from the ruckus, bent over and coughed the dust from his lungs and wiped it from his eyes. When he stood up he saw the stare of the shaman as he angrily asked, "What did you do?"

Tatum gave his most innocent look as he said, "Me? Why, nothin', it just caved in an' I'm lucky to get out alive!"

CHAPTER THIRTY-ONE
ESCAPE

DUSK HAD GIVEN WAY TO DARKNESS WHEN TATUM HEARD A scratching at the entry flap. He pushed it aside to see a boy of about twelve summers motioning to the rear of the lodge. Tatum stepped into the darkness and walked around the lodge to see both his horses and two others tethered together in the darkness, no more than three paces from the tepee. Tatum looked to the boy, saw another of the same age at his side and nodded his head in thanks and watched the boys disappear into the night.

He stepped into the dim light of the lodge, the only illumination coming from a small central fire, and whispered to the sisters, "I'm going to saddle the horses and put the packs on the bay. It'll take a few moments, and I'll scratch at the entry for you to come out. While I do that, move all the blankets back, put on those new buckskins White Feather gave you, and be ready."

Both girls eagerly nodded their heads and bent to their work while Tatum exited the lodge to start rigging the horses.

They led the horses from the part of the village that

remained. With many lodges moved in the past weeks to the distant camp, there were few remaining, mostly of close relatives of the afflicted. The darkness covered their movements and they were careful to be as quiet as possible but as they started to mount, White Feather stepped from the black and said, "I am sorry to see you go, but it is best. I hope that someday you will return."

Tatum looked at the woman who had become both friend and teacher and replied, "Someday, I will. You have been a good friend, White Feather, and be sure to tell your father thank you."

"My father knows and has said that we are in your debt. You will always be a friend to the Comanche," she said as she handed him a beaded belt. "This will tell other Comanche that you are a friend of our people." He looked at the belt with a myriad of designs made from quills and colored beads and said, "Thank you, White Feather."

He motioned to the sisters to mount up and he swung aboard the sorrel. He reached down and took White Feather's hand and said, "Good bye, my friend." She smiled and stepped back as the trio started on the same trail that led Tatum to the camp so many days ago. He twisted in his seat and stood in his stirrups to look back, but the darkness hid everything from his view. With a deep sigh, he settled into his saddle and let the sorrel have his head to follow the dim trail along the small creek and to the dark timber. By the time they reached the deep timber, he knew the moon would be out and the clear night sky would show off the bright stars and the trail would be easily followed.

This was familiar country and Tatum held the rimrock ridge over his left shoulder and the row of three slide-rock covered peaks as landmarks to his right. They were in the bottom of a wide draw between the two ridges that followed a small willow-lined creek. The trail kept about twenty to thirty yards from the creek but occasionally the chuckle of the white water as it cascaded over the rocks would filter its way to the travelers. Tatum was comforted by the sounds of the night that were so familiar to him, but the women tried to stay as close to Tatum as possible, fearful of the strange sounds and sights of the darkness.

It was close to midnight when the trail came to the confluence of the creek beside them and the Cucharas creek that marked the end of the rimrock ridge that had been their protector for the first part of the night. As they came into the clearing, the moon was bright, and their eyes had become accustomed to the dim light. But just the openness of the wider meadow and the crossing of the Cucharas seemed to lift the spirits of the girls and they spoke above a whisper for the first time since they left the village.

When a coyote barked and lifted his cry to the stars, both girls were startled and nudged their horses nearer the sorrel and Val asked Tatum, "Is that a wolf?"

He chuckled before he answered, "No, that's just a coyote calling his girlfriend."

Her shoulders visibly dropped as she relaxed and said, "We've heard coyotes before, but never this close."

"There's nothing to be concerned about unless you're a cottontail rabbit. Then they might chase you down, but I don't think you need to worry."

To join in the conversation a great horned owl asked his age-old question and Cat said, "Oh, that's Mr. Owl. I never heard him so clear before."

Tatum was pleased to see the girls starting to relax and with the trail moving across the flats near the creek bottom, they rode side by side and began to converse freely. Val asked Tatum, "So, what are we going to do now?"

Tatum looked at both girls and said, "Well, I guess that's up to you. Do you think you want to go on to California?"

"How could we do that? Or anything else, for that matter?" asked Cat.

"Well, my pa used to always say ya gotta look to see what the problem is, then figger out how to solve the problem, then get busy doin' it."

"Well, we really haven't had much time to talk about it or even think about it. We don't have any money or anything else for that matter. So, I don't know," said Val, then looked at her sister and asked, "What do you think, Cat?"

"I don't know. Before all this happened, all we thought about was going to California, starting a vineyard and someday getting married and have a family. We never thought about much else, but I guess we oughta."

"Well, ladies, all we gotta think about now is finding us a camp. Come first light, I'd like us to be settled into a camp so I can hunt us up some fresh meat and we can have us a good meal. How's that sound?"

Both girls answered in the affirmative with nodding heads and a unison 'yes' followed by a giggle, the first Tatum had heard in several weeks, and he thought it sure added to the sounds of the night that had been his comfort for so long.

It was a good stand of cottonwood surrounded by ample willows and alder and chokecherry that gave shelter, cover and graze for the animals. Before first light showed in the east, their camp was made with bedrolls laid out and a small fire started with a coffeepot sitting nearby. While traveling with the wagon train, the girls had a few routine chores, but their cooking was mostly helping their mothers and learning as they worked. Now, those lessons had to be applied, but supplies were different than the ample provisions of the wagons. Tatum had stocked up for one man, but for an extended period, and his supplies were sufficient. But the pots and pans were not as sizable as those the girls had used with their mothers. And the additional provender was limited to what was available around them and not like they were used to, just reaching into the stores in the wagon.

Cat looked at Tatum as he poured himself a cup of coffee and said, "Uh, we looked at the supplies, and you've got corn-meal, flour, sugar and stuff, but no other food items. You know, like potatoes and things." Her pleading tone made the statement into a question and he let a smile slowly split his face as he realized the girls weren't used to gathering food in the wild. He nodded his head and said, "Well, I was about to go lookin' for some meat so I guess you two could tag along, if you're quiet that is, and I'll show you a few things that'll go with the meat for cookin' an' such."

They looked at him with both faces showing a question, and Val asked, "What do you mean, you'll show us a few things?"

"You know, things to eat and that you can cook with the meat, like a stew."

"Here?" asked Cat as she looked around their camp.

"Well, not right here, but as we go lookin' around, we'll find things."

"I'm not sure I can eat whatever it is you're talking about," said Val.

Tatum laughed at the girls and asked, "And just what do you think you've been eating for the last couple of weeks?"

The girls looked at each other and realized their foolishness and laughed with Tatum. They sat down on nearby large stones and shared the only other coffee cup. When Tatum tossed the dregs aside, they stood to join him on the hunt.

As they moved beside the willows and the stream, when-ever Tatum spotted something usable, he pointed it out and showed the girls how to identify each item. By the time they returned to camp, the girls had hands full of Yampa roots, cat-tail roots, wild onions, and strawberries and raspberries. Tatum carried a fat turkey and grinned as the girls jabbered on about their wilderness education. He breathed deep, and let his shoulders slowly sag as he thought about the challenges that faced them. He certainly hadn't planned on having company with him as he carved out his place in the mountains, but he wasn't sure what he could do with the sisters. In the meantime, he supposed he would just have to take one day at a time and teach them what he could, and learn what he didn't know. He had often wondered what it would be like to have a sister or even a girlfriend but this was the last place he needed either one.

He fashioned a spit for the turkey to be cooked over the fire while the girls prepared the gathered vegetables. The strawberries and raspberries were slowly disappearing as wandering hands found the pile of sweets that were set aside for later. While everything was cooking, Tatum watched the girls as they puttered about the camp, tending to the cooking and arranging things to their satisfaction. He enjoyed watching them and just having the time to themselves. He didn't think anyone from the Comanche village would pursue them, certain that Buffalo Hump would stop any effort by Spirit Talker for any kind of vengeance, but he took a stroll around the camp just for his own peace of mind.

CHAPTER THIRTY-TWO
CONSIDERATIONS

SOMETHING HAD AWAKENED HIM, BUT HE DID NOT MOVE although he scanned the camp and surrounding area as best as the moonlight would allow and what he could see without moving. The horses stood with heads up and ears forward; something had caught their attention as well, but nothing so alarming that they were spooked. That told Tatum it wasn't a dangerous animal that would make the horses nervous, but probably a man or men that did not frighten them but made them curious. His hand grasped the butt of his Paterson and the other he held to his tomahawk. Still covered by his blankets, he casually rolled to his back to give himself a better view in the direction of the horses' stare. He saw a shadow, the hunched form of a man, slip from one bunch of sage to another, closer to the camp. Whoever he was, he was moving slowly and carefully and as Tatum watched, the form lifted and started for a tree at the edge of the clearing and at the same instant Tatum slipped from his blankets to gain the cover of the logs near the fire ring. The coals had diminished to nothing but ashes and gave no light to reveal Tatum's hiding place.

The figure stepped from behind the tree and approached the camp, but Tatum saw no weapon but didn't trust anyone that would try to sneak into a camp of sleeping people. He waited as the figure came closer and spoke, "That's far enough!" The tone of his voice was firm but not alarming, and the figure froze in place. Tatum started to rise from behind the log and a familiar voice said, "Long Bow? Is that you?"

Tatum recognized the voice and answered, "Yes, White Feather. Why are you here?" he asked as he rose to his full height, dropping his hand with the Colt to his side.

"I have come to warn you there is trouble coming," she explained as she came nearer.

Tatum motioned for her to be seated on one of the logs as he picked up some firewood and fed the still hot coals; he fanned the coals until a tongue of flame licked at the fresh fuel and he sat back to look at his visitor.

"So, what is this trouble?"

She dropped her head and lifted it again as she began to explain, "Spirit Talker was upset when he found you gone and wanted to have some warriors to follow you and bring you back so he could destroy you. Buffalo Hump refused him and said you were a friend to the people. Spirit Talker was not pleased and still wants you dead. He blames you for the death of Black Bull."

"Is that all there is? Or is it just to show his power?"

"Many of our people are thankful for what you have done, and they agree with Buffalo Hump. Spirit Talker thinks they believe you are more powerful than he, and he must prove that he has special favor with the Great Spirit. But there is more. The man that attacked you, White Horse, his father is the brother of Spirit Talker's father. Spirit Talker left the camp, and Badger said he had talked with White Horse, but Spirit Talker denied that because it is against our custom."

Tatum nodded his head in understanding and said, "So, you think maybe Spirit Talker had told White Horse to come after me? But I don't think White Horse needed any encouragement to do that; I've been expecting him to come after me anyway. When I saw you coming, I thought maybe you were White Horse."

Their conversation, though in muted tones, and the increased light from the fire, stirred the sisters to wakefulness and when they saw White Feather, they rose from their blankets and came to join in the morning discussion. They were alarmed at the news of the pursuit of White Horse, and Cat looked to Tatum and asked, "So, what do we do? I know he's only one, but still . . . "

"I know, we'll move our camp and take all the precautions necessary. We'll be alright, I promise," he said as he did his best to reassure the sisters. He felt they had already endured more than most and he didn't want any more challenges forced upon them. He looked at White Feather. "Thanks for coming to warn us. Now that the light's coming," and he nodded to the dim grey in the east, "we'll have us something to eat, and we'll move our camp. Coffee'll be ready in a bit, and you need something to eat before you travel back to your village. Won't you stay?"

"No," and she placed her hand on his arm and added, "we are moving the village as you said. The shaman will be busy today with the burial of Black Bull; I think he's going to burn the body with the rest of the things. I think he's afraid of it all, but I must help my father. May the Spirit keep you safe." She stood and walked back to her horse that was tethered away from the camp. Tatum followed a short way and watched her leave, thankful for her warning and wondering about their next move.

As he returned to the fire, he saw the expectant faces of

the sisters watching him and he smiled and said, "So, you got the coffee ready yet?"

His simple question spurred the girls to action and took their thoughts off what could be impending danger. They busied themselves with their preparations of the leftover biscuits and stew from the night before. The coffee wafted its aroma to tempt Tatum and he reached for the pot to pour himself some of the dark brew. He sat back and looked at the busy sisters and asked, "So, have you two given much thought to what you want to do? You know, about your future?"

They stopped what they were doing and looked at Tatum and Val said, "Well, we've talked about some things, but nothing definite. The only relative we have left, at least here in America, is our mother's sister back in Maryland. She and her husband were going to come to California with us, but when her husband passed away, she didn't think she could make the trip by herself. She took their savings and opened a dress shop. So, we don't really know yet. But we'll talk more and think and pray about it. I'm sure we'll decide soon."

Tatum had listened carefully, thinking as she spoke, and waited a moment, finished his coffee and said, "Ladies, there's no real hurry. You take your time and whatever you decide, we'll work it out somehow. But for now, let's put this camp behind us as soon as possible and make for a better place just in case."

Tatum had given considerable thought to the future of the sisters and believed the best place for them to be when they decided their future would be at Bent's Fort. If they chose to continue to California, their best possibility of joining a wagon train headed west would be at the fort. Many trains came through the fort, with some taking the Sante Fe Trail to the south or the northern route of the Old Spanish Trail to the west and on to California. That was the route their families wagon train was following before they were left in the valley. But if the sisters chose to return to the east, they might be able to travel with a trader's caravan back to St. Louis and on from there. As he considered the options, and the possibility of pursuit from White Horse and perhaps others, he chose to continue on the trail along the Cucharas River that would eventually take them to the Arkansas and Bent's Fort. He remembered the valley of the Cucharas had considerable tree cover and several wooded knolls that would be suitable for a better and more defensible camp and every mile would take them closer to Bent's Fort.

Tatum led the way trailing his packhorse and the sisters followed close behind. The trail was wide enough to allow them to travel side by side and the women took advantage of the time to discuss their future, seeming to talk continuously as they rocked in the saddle, totally unconcerned about their surroundings and lost in their conversation. Tatum looked over his shoulder to occasionally watch the trail behind them and chuckled at their complete immersion in their discussion. He began to plan for their camp and possible attack by the renegade White Horse.

He reached well back into his past and the times in the woods with his friend Red Calf. The two had often set snares for game and even for each other as they honed their skills in the woods, and maybe some of those tricks might be used against White Horse. He began to map out in his mind a location for the camp, high up on a knoll, well hidden in the trees and with few approaches. Approaches that could be set with snares or traps or at least something that would give them warning. His horses were a definite asset with their superior hearing and attention, but he needed a greater advantage. He knew in his last battle with the renegade he was lucky for White Horse was a proven warrior and Tatum had few contests where his life hung in the balance. So it was important to swing the scales in his favor.

He searched the terrain before him and saw the ridge-marked bluff to his left that held a scattering of juniper and pinion, several outcroppings of stone and assorted cacti. The bluff rose from the flats of the river bottom and offered a vantage point, but little cover. To his right, the thicker cottonwood and undergrowth gave cover but that same cover protected an attacker and with no clear field of view, the renegade could be upon them without warning. Before him, where the bluff faded back, a sizable timber covered knoll caught his attention and he stood in his stirrups to give it a once-over. It appeared to be just what he had envisioned for their camp: good cover, little access and, if they camped there, they would have the high ground.

He dropped into his seat and started to turn to tell the sisters when suddenly a thunder of hooves came from the creek-side trees and before he could turn to face the threat, the renegade charged his horse directly into the front shoulder of the sorrel, knocking him to the side and down, throwing Tatum into the dirt. He rolled free from the horse and grabbed for his Paterson Colt, but it was gone! He spat dust and wiped dirt from his face and eyes just as White Horse leapt from his horse and, screaming his war cry, landed atop Tatum. White Horse held a knife and lifted it with rage in his eyes as he screamed again, and started to drop the knife to plunge it into Tatum's chest. But Tatum grabbed the wrist with the knife and pushed it aside as the renegade forced his other hand to the white man's throat. Tatum squirmed and bucked to loosen the grip of the Indian, and slid out from under him.

Once free, Tatum grabbed for his tomahawk and his Bowie knife and with one in each hand, the two combatants began to circle one another. Both in a slight crouch, hands held out to the side and staring into one another's eyes, the malevolence of the Indian brought forth another scream as he lunged toward Tatum, knife swooping from his right to his left. Tatum sucked in his gut and arched his back as he tiptoed, causing the blade to cut his buckskin shirt, but not his skin. As the knife swooped past, Tatum brought his hawk down across the arm of White Horse, and drew blood but only from a superficial wound.

The Indian spun around and lifted his leg as he spun, hoping to connect with the head of Tatum, but just the flat of his foot grazed his face. Tatum staggered back and the Indian pressed his advantage, lunging forward, missing, but on the return, brought the blade of his knife across the side of Tatum. The white man felt the burning at his side, and knew he was bleeding but he never let his eyes leave the Indian. Tatum knew he was on the defensive, but remembered Tallchief telling him the attacker always had the advantage, and he knew he had to take the fight to his adversary.

Back in their crouches and circling, the Indian spat curses at his hated enemy, and Tatum understood some of the words, but focused on the moves rather than the words of the Indian. He watched as the warrior would move to his right, pause, feint with the knife and immediately move back to his left. Again, with the same move, and after the feint, Tatum dropped to his knee and swung the hawk to the knee of the Indian and scored a direct hit that buckled the knee and brought the Indian down. Tatum sprang forward with the Bowie and swiped across the shoulder of White Horse with a deep cut that brought a grimace and a scream.

Tatum stepped back out of reach of White Horse's knife, and watched the Indian drop to hands and knees but lift his head and snarl at Tatum. He searched for his knife, found it and came up in a charge. Tatum was unprepared, thinking the Indian would start the circling and taunting again, and when White Horse came flying at him, he was tackled and the two fell to the ground with White Horse atop Tatum. The Indian sat up and his rage of vengeance forced him to watch the face of his enemy as he killed him. But that second of rage gave Tatum his opportunity and he brought his Bowie up and into the side of White Horse whose face twisted in alarm and anger as he grabbed at his side and felt the hot blood pump over his hand. Tatum swung his hawk broadside and struck White Horse above his ear, knocking the renegade from his perch on Tatum's chest.

But hatred, anger, and vengeance gave strength to the wounded Indian as he rolled away from his enemy, came to one knee, spewed threats from between clenched teeth, and struggled to his feet in a crouch. He still held one hand at his wound on his side, but the other held the knife and he screamed and charged at the hated white man. Tatum waited until the last second, feinted to the right and stepped to the left as the charging Indian stumbled forward, and Tatum brought his hawk down on the neck of the renegade as he passed. Tatum held tight to his hawk, and the blade made a sucking sound and it pulled from the severed muscles at the side of the renegade's neck as he dropped face down in the dirt.

Tatum turned to watch the figure fall, and stepped back. He watched, mesmerized, as the dust slowly rose in small clouds from the prone figure, now motionless. The silence was broken when Cat and Val walked to his side and Cat said, "I was so afraid for you, but it all happened so fast." The sisters looked at their protector, saw the blood at his side and Val said, "You're hurt, let us help you."

Tatum looked down at his side; blood covered the left side of his buckskin britches, a slit in the tunic showed his bloody side and he saw blood still coming from the cut. He put his hand to his side, pulling the remnants of his shirt to block the blood flow, and looking at the girls said, "Maybe we should make camp," and nodded his head toward the trees by the creek. "How 'bout over there?" As they looked where he indicated, they saw a small clearing and turned back to see Tatum prone in the dirt.

CHAPTER THIRTY-THREE
TENDING

WHEN TATUM AWOKE, HE WAS ON HIS BEDROLL NEAR A SMALL fire and he smelled coffee. He struggled to sit up, and felt the stabbing pain in his side. He looked down and saw a blood-soaked bandage held at his side with a rawhide thong wrapped around his middle. He started to reach for a cup and the coffee, but was stopped by the stern voice of Caterina that said, "Sit still, I'll get your coffee." She came from behind him and reached down for the pot, poured a cup of steaming black coffee and handed it to Tatum as he squirmed to make himself more comfortable. Cat sat across from him and said, "We're going to have to do something about that cut, and I'm not sure what to do. Any ideas?"

Tatum took a sip of the hot brew and looked up at the young woman who showed concern as she looked sympathetically at her friend. "I dunno. How deep is it?"

"It's not real deep, but we can't get it to stop bleeding. I've seen cuts sewn with thread but we don't have any, do we?"

"I've got something that would work if we need it but, if it's not so deep, maybe just cauterize it. I'd have to look at it to see." He sat his cup down and lifted his arm to look at the bandage. He started tugging at it and was stopped by Cat. "Stop it! I'll take it off, just sit still." She came to his side, pushed him back against the log and began removing the bandage. She daubed at the wound and looked up at Tatum and said, "Now you can look at it."

He lifted his arm and bent his head down to see as much of the wound as he could, poked at it to see the depth of the cut and examined it as best he could. Cat had to daub at the blood as it continued to seep from the wound. He looked up at her and said, "I think if you cauterize it, it'll be okay."

"And just how do we do that?" asked Val as she came from the horses. Although it seemed like they had been camped for some time, it was no more than an hour and Val had picketed the horses close to the edge of the creek, affording them access to both water and graze.

"Well, I've never done it, but I've seen it done," and he twisted to slip his Bowie knife from the sheath at his belt. "First, you'll need to get this red hot, and then you'll need to apply it to the cut to seal it off." He lifted his eyebrows and looked at the girls as they stood side-by-side and looked at him. They looked at one another and Cat said, "Not me!" and lifted her hands up as she shook her head. Val looked at her sister, exasperated, and said, "Then you'll have to help."

"Help? How?" she asked, wide-eyed.

"Do you really think he'll be able to sit still while I burn his side with a hot knife?"

"You mean . . ." started Cat as she looked at Tatum and then at his wound, pointing.

"Yup," said Tatum, grinning. "It's gonna hurt like all git out, and I'll need something or someone to hang on to. I can't go movin' when she's puttin' the hot knife to me or she's liable to put it clear through!"

Cat looked at them both, dropped her hands and started walking back and forth as if she needed to work up the courage. She appeared to be talking to herself as she had one hand on her hip and the other waving in the air. She stopped and looked at Tatum and said, "Are you sure?" He grinned up at her and replied, "Believe me, if there was some other way, I'd do it." She let out a heavy sigh and said, "Alright, let's do it 'fore he loses what blood he's got left."

Tatum stuck the knife blade into the fire and said, "You might wanna put a wet rag of some sort over the handle so it don't get too hot," and began scooting down to lie prone. He rolled to his side, exposing his wounded side for the girls to have access. Cat got to her knees behind him and sat back on her heels as they waited for the knife to heat. Tatum said, "I'm gonna put this," motioning to the knife scabbard in his hand, "in my mouth, but I'll probably still make a noise. Don't let it bother you, just hold me down anyway. When I saw this done before, the fella passed out and didn't come around for a spell so if that happens, don't worry none."

Val asked, "When I do this, do I use the edge in the cut or . . ."

"No, use the flat of the blade, like you're sealing it up. Oh, and it's gonna stink." He grinned as he watched their reaction and chuckled at their wrinkled noses. He thought the scars from the pox on their faces were fading and that these sisters really were quite pretty. He looked at the fire and the knife's blade was beginning to glow a dull orange and he said, "I think it's ready. Are you?" as he looked at Val. She nodded and scooted on her knees closer beside him. She looked at the wound, motioned for Cat to daub at the bleeding, and turned to retrieve the knife. She held it with both hands as she turned to her task, glanced at Tatum who had the scabbard in his teeth and saw him nod at her, then look away.

Val slowly moved the blade to the wound, took a deep breath and inched closer and closer. The heat of the blade touched the fine hair at his side and it sizzled and startled the girl who drew back. She let out her breath, took another, and started toward the wound again. In a smooth motion, the blade touched the back part of the wound, sizzled, and smoke and stench rose. But the girls did not flinch, and Val drew the blade across the wound and the searing continued. Tatum groaned and as Val lifted the blade, she saw Tatum relax and the knife scabbard drop from his teeth. She looked at him, fearful, but saw he was breathing evenly and she sat back and looked at her sister and nodded her head. Both women sat back on their heels and visibly relaxed in relief.

After examining the wound and seeing the blistered result of the cauterization, Cat nodded to Val and said, "The bleedings stopped, but this looks horrible. I hope it works." She pulled a blanket up to his shoulder as Val lifted his head and placed another folded blanket for a pillow. The ladies poured themselves a cup of coffee and looked across the fire at one another. Val smiled and said, "Did you ever dream we would be alone out in this wilderness and doing what we just did?"

Cat chuckled and said, "No, and you didn't either."

They finished their coffee and set to work with the usual camp duties of fixing the meal and laying out the bedrolls. They continued their discussions as to their future plans and had resumed their seats by the fire when Tatum stirred awake. His groan caught their attention and they looked at their patient, watching him push back the blanket and twist around to look at the wound. The sisters had thought it best to not replace a bandage, and give the wound time to dry out and start to scab. Tatum looked up at the women and said, "Thanks ladies, I think."

They giggled at his remark and said, "Well, supper's ready, if you think you're hungry."

"Yup, I'm hungry alright. And whatever you've got cookin' is smellin' powerful good." Val went to their patient and helped him sit up and lean back against the log to be in a more comfortable position to eat. Cat brought him a plate of stew and biscuits and a cup of coffee that she sat beside him. He looked at both the ladies and grinned as he sat the plate on his lap and started eating. They fixed their own plates and sat nearby, and Tatum said, "We might need to stay here for a day or two till I'm ready to ride. But you ladies might have to round us up some fresh meat...if you think you can, that is."

They looked at one another and Val said, "You mean, us, go hunting?"

"Well, I don't think any self respectin' deer's gonna walk into camp and say, 'shoot me', do you?"

Val looked at Tatum with disbelief written on her face as she exclaimed, "I've never even shot a gun much less killed a living thing!"

"Me neither!" echoed Cat.

Tatum chuckled at their response, knowing they had a good amount of smoked elk meat in the parfleche, but he knew the women were unaware of his supply. He said, "Well, guess we're gonna get mighty hungry these next few days. And me, a wounded man, needing fresh meat an' all." He shook his head, keeping the most serious expression on his face he could muster as he looked sorrowfully at the women.

They finished their meal, did the clean-up and turned in for the night. It promised to be a clear night with a big moon and bright stars and no more concern about pursuing rene-gades. The sisters had retrieved Tatum's Paterson and he had it by his side with his tomahawk. They lay near one another and looked at the stars as they talked about their future.

Val began with, "We've talked about what to do, and we're thinkin' our only hope is to go back to Aunt Isabella's. We thought about going on to California, but the vines are gone and . . ." Tatum interrupted, "The vines are not gone. The wagon they were in didn't burn, and I planted them near the graves of your family. I don't know if they'll live, but I watered them and they looked healthy when I planted them."

The girls turned to look at Tatum and at one another, but Val continued, "Thank you, Tate. That was good of you. But still, we wouldn't be able to start a vineyard like our father would. Only the men worked in the vineyard and we wouldn't know what to do." She let a little snicker escape as she said, "I remember the girls and the women when the harvest of the grapes came. We would stomp the grapes to get the juice; there would be music and laughter and feasting. It was great fun, but we—the two of us—could not do all that would have to be done."

Cat chimed in, "Aunt Isabella has a big place and there would be room for us. We might even learn to be dressmakers."

Val said softly, "After what you did with our families and the others, I thought I might want to learn to be a nurse and help others."

Tatum lay quietly and listened to the girls, picturing them in the city with their aunt and when Val spoke of being a nurse, he turned to look at them. "Well, ladies, we won't leave here for a day or two and, even then, there's still time to think about it. So whatever you decide, I'll do my best to help you."

Cat said just above a whisper but still loud enough to understand, "Thank you Tatum, for everything."

CHAPTER THIRTY-FOUR
LEARNING

TATUM'S FRUSTRATION WITH HIS INACTIVITY DURING HIS recuperation found an outlet as he began teaching the sisters about guns. Using his rifle and pistol, he gave them lessons on how to load with the correct measure of powder, place the patch and ball, seat them and ram them down with the wiping rod. With the pistol, he showed how to load the cylinder as they did the Hawken, only with less amounts, smaller patch and balls and using the loading lever to seat the balls. He carefully instructed them with the percussion caps and in the cautionary handling of the weapons. As they learned, they became anxious to learn more and how to shoot. Tatum felt they were safe from discovery by any hostiles and he condescended to some practical instruction. Val was the first to try the Hawken and after properly loading and priming, she listened closely as Tatum talked her through the lifting, seating the butt firmly against her shoulder, and how to line up the rear buckhorn with the front blade sight. He showed her about the setting of the rear trigger and cautioned her about the front trigger. When he thought she was ready, he walked her through the steps again and as she had her sight picture, he said, "Now take in a breath, let a little out, and slowly squeeze the front trigger."

The sudden explosion rocked her back on her heels and she caught her balance with one foot behind her and let the rifle barrel drop towards the ground. She was so startled, she didn't even look at her target that was partially obscured by the grey smoke. She looked at Tatum and he laughed, as did Cat, and he pointed toward the target which was a piece of cottonwood bark with a black circle made with charcoal. She looked and saw the bark lying in pieces in front of the log that had previously held it erect. She looked back at Tatum and excitedly said, "I hit it!"

Tatum and Cat couldn't stop laughing but he nodded his head in agreement and looked at Val as she looked from the target to her observers and began to laugh with them. "You didn't tell me it was so loud, and it almost knocked me over!" Her remark elicited another round of laughter and they all enjoyed the comedic relief.

Cat took her turn but knew what to expect and flinched as she pulled the trigger, making her miss the target. But both girls did well with additional tries and Tatum was especially pleased with their innate skill with the pistol. They finished their practice and Tatum returned to his blankets for some more recuperation. His side was healing well, but he had lost a considerable amount of blood and was still a little weak. As he took to his blankets, he said, "I think maybe we'll be able to get back on the trail in the morning. We can take it easy, but I've had enough of this layin' around." The girls nodded their approval and said they would let him rest while they went to gather some more plants for their supper. He cautioned, "Take the pistol with you, just to be safe."

When he awoke, it was to the crackling sound of meat cooking in the pan near the flames. He sat up to look into the pan and saw two fat trout cooking in the pan. He saw Cat tending the pan and looked at her with a question on his face and she smiled as she said, "We already knew how to catch fish; we've done a lot of fishing in our time. Hungry?" she asked as she looked at the bewildered expression on Tatum's face. He nodded his head wordlessly and looked around for the other sister. Cat again anticipated his question and said, "She took the horses farther downstream for some better graze. She'll be back in a minute." He saw three more trout, already cooked, sitting on a plate near the fire keeping warm. Another pot was filled with an assortment of vegetables gathered by the girls and was also sitting back from the flames, awaiting the group meal. Tatum looked up when he heard Val call, "Supper ready?" as she came into the clearing. Tatum was amazed at the change in the sisters. Where before they were withdrawn and quiet, now they showed a confidence and assurance Tatum had not seen before. He shook his head and rolled from his blankets to take a seat on the log. He poured himself a cup of coffee and watched as Val came near and sat on the large stone opposite Tatum. She smiled at him and said, "The horses had pretty well eaten everything where they were so I moved them to another small clearing downstream a little. I'll bring them back before we turn in."

He nodded his head in understanding, took a sip of coffee and looked from one sister to the other. He said, "I was just thinking about how much the two of you have changed."

"Changed? What do you mean?" asked Cat as she filled plates and passed them to Tatum and her sister.

"Well, before, you two were quiet and all. But now you act like you're right at home."

"Thanks to you, we are," said Val. "Now, are you gonna pray for this meal so we can eat?"

Tatum chuckled and said "Sure," and spoke a simple prayer to give thanks and to ask for God's continued protection. As he said, "Amen," the girls echoed him and began to chatter about their decision.

"That sounds to me like you've made up your minds then," said Tatum.

"Well, we thought about the other two options and decided that going back to our Aunt Isabella's would be best," said Val, grinning.

Tatum looked at her, wrinkled his brow, and asked, "Two options? I thought you were just considering California or your aunt's. What's the other option?"

Val grinned and said, "Well, we talked about both of us staying out here with you, you know, both of us marryin' up with you like they did back in old times, but . . . "

Tatum spit out his mouth full of food as he choked on what she said, and before he could speak she continued, "But we thought you were too young to handle two wives so we're going to go to our aunt's." She fought to keep a straight face, but Cat couldn't hold it any longer and busted out in laughter that caught Val in its tide and both girls were laughing and pointing at Tatum's expression of disbelief. He finally realized they had put one over on him and he finally let a smile split his face and laughter rise up and join the fun.

Everyone was more relaxed than they had been in weeks. The decision was made; now it was a matter of formulating their course of action. Tatum explained, "Bent's Fort is kind of a jumping off place for a lot of trade caravan's that come through. There are several traders that come out of St. Louis and take freight wagons full of goods to Sante Fe and trade for hides and such that they bring back to St. Louis. And sometimes, there's folks that have changed their plans and leave the wagon trains and go back to their farms and most of them pass through the Fort to get supplies. Now, I'm thinkin' you could probably join up with one or 'tother, and get yourself a ride back east to your aunt's."

"But won't we have to pay our way?" asked Cat.

"Not necessarily. You might have to work your way, you know, helpin' out with cookin' and such like. But folks are usually pretty understandin' and helpful."

"But what if we can't find anybody going back east?" asked Val.

Tatum grinned and said, "Well, there's always the other option."

Both girls laughed at him and looked for something to throw, but found nothing and were satisfied with laughter. Tatum added, "Don't go worryin' none about it. It'll all work out, I'm sure."

The girls looked at one another and shrugged their shoulders as they started the clean-up and making ready for the night. Tatum had explained the Fort was still several days away and they needed to get an early start. When they turned in, they looked at the canopy of stars and the three-quartered moon and each pondered their own quiet thoughts as they drifted off to sleep.

CHAPTER THIRTY-FIVE
FORT

IT WAS LATE ON THE FOURTH DAY ON THE TRAIL WHEN BENT'S Fort came into sight of the trio of travelers. It had been an enjoyable and interesting four days. Val used Tatum's Hawken and dropped a small buck on their second morning, but both women had a difficult time with the gutting and skinning of the deer. Cat said if it was alright with everyone else, she would stick to cooking and let the rest of it be done by Tatum and Val. The four days had been spent in pleasant conversation, learning about the terrain and each other, and sharing dreams of the future. Val had spoken more about the possibility of learning about nursing, knowing the only way to become a nurse was similar to an apprenticeship program.

Society was still struggling with educating women and even more with the idea of women in any type of career role. Medicine was strictly limited to men, except in the role of helper, like a nurse. But Val's mind had become more set on the idea, always remembering the aid Tatum had given to the hopeless suffering Comanche and to her family and friends. Tatum would occasionally catch her looking at him with a wistful expression and would ask, "What?" but she would only shake her head and smile. She was remembering how Rosa's mother and Rosa herself had referred to Tatum as a saint and she was beginning to think they were right. She had a sudden thought and asked, "Tate, you never told us your last name, did you?"

"I don't recall. Why? Is it important to you?"

"Just wonderin', that's all. If we go back east like we're planning, I might like to write you a letter and I need to know who to send it to, don't I?" asked Val, looking at her sister who nodded her head in agreement.

"So, our last name is LaBella. What's yours?" asked Cat.

"Well, a long time ago when our family left the Isle of Man in the British Isles and came to America, our family name was Saint Michaels. But when my grandfather reached America, he shortened it to Saint."

The sisters looked at one another and Val let a grin slowly cross her face and she replied, "Tate Saint. Somehow that's fitting. Tate Saint; yes, it is."

The ford at the Arkansas led them across a gravelly bottom and water no more than belly deep on the horses, making for an easy crossing. As the horses climbed the sloping bank, each one stopped and shook, causing the women to grab the saddle horns and clutch with their legs as they giggled at the rolling shake of their mounts.

The gates to the fort stood open and people were walking in and out. Val and Cat were surprised to see the many tepees of the Cheyenne camped near the fort and so many of them walking about the fort. Reassured by Tatum, they soon lost interest and scanned the interior of the massive adobe structure. Tatum reined up in front of the trader's door, stepped down and tethered his horses. He motioned for the girls to join him and they quickly followed suit. When he stepped into the trader's store, he stopped and let his eyes adjust to the darkened interior, lit only by the fading light coming in the single window and two lanterns hanging from the support posts.

As Tatum looked around, he remembered his first time here and his brief confrontation with the big drunk, Smitty. He also thought of Carson and Bent and looked up as the trader said, "Welcome, stranger. Say, ain't I seen you afore?"

Tatum grinned as he stepped closer to the counter and the trader and replied, "Yessir, I was in here a couple months ago. Is Carson or Bent around?"

"Oh, yeah, I 'member you. You was the kid that got ol' Smitty to sober up," and chuckled, "but's far as Carson's concerned, he's long gone. Went up north to see some o' them 'rapaho. But Bent's around. William is anyway. He's o'er yonder at his place. It's the place in the corner thar. Just rap on the door, he'll let you in."

"Thank you, sir. Oh, by the way, do you know of any trader caravan comin' back through or wagon trains goin' east?" asked Tatum.

"Whatsamatta, you quittin' the mountains already?"

"No, it's for the ladies here. They need to get back to the city and they're gonna be needin' to join up with somebody. I thought maybe some o' them freighters or somethin'."

"Wal, as I think on it, ol' McKenzie's outfit's due just about any day now. They'll be goin' back to St. Louie. That might work fer ya. 'Sides, ol' McKenzie allus has his woman with him an' she cooks fer the crew. I'm thinkin' she'd like sum comp'ny."

Tatum grinned at the news and looked at the girls to see if they heard what the trader had said, but the expressions on their faces told the story of their excitement at the possibility. He motioned for them to come outside with him and he led them to the door of William Bent's quarters. He lifted his hand to rap on the door but before his fist fell, the door swung wide and a startled William Bent stepped back, not expecting to be confronted by someone at his doorway.

Tatum spoke up, "Mr. Bent," and stretching out his hand he continued, "I'm Tatum Saint, I was here . . ." but was interrupted by Bent with an uplifted hand as he said, "Hold on there. What are you doing in my doorway and who did you say you were?"

"I'm sorry, I didn't mean to alarm you. I'm Tatum Saint. I met you a couple of months ago here with Kit Carson."

Bent stepped back and shaded his eyes as he looked at the man in front of him. His face visibly relaxed as he recognized Tatum and he said, "Oh yeah, I remember, you're the kid that stopped Smitty. Yeah, so, what're you doin' now? You're not leavin' the mountains already are you? Carson thought sure you'd be one o' 'em what stuck it out."

"No, sir, I'm not leaving the mountains. But I do have a couple ladies with me that could use some help," he said as he stepped aside to reveal Cat and Val. Bent looked at the ladies and said, "Now, how'd you find two young ladies in these mountains? You know, there's been many a man wants to find themselves a lady in these mountains but ain't none of 'em ever done it. And now you come up with two! Glory be! Well, don't just stand there, come on in an' tell me all about it," he ordered as he stepped back from the doorway.

Bent invited them to stay for dinner, introduced them to his wife, Owl Woman of the Cheyenne, and sat them all down to hear their story. As Tatum began, William Bent settled into his big chair made from the antlers of several elk, lit his pipe and gave the trio his attention.

Tatum wasn't a storyteller and, as he spoke, the sisters found it necessary to add the details that he often left out and

Bent chuckled at their relay way of telling the story. His attention heightened as he listened, surprised about the plague and especially at their peaceful stay with the Comanche. He knew of Buffalo Hump but had never met him nor had any dealings with him or his people. As Tatum brought the tale to an end, he finished with, "And we were hoping you'd help the ladies get back to St. Louis or even to Massachusetts and their aunt."

Bent leaned forward, rested his elbows on his knees, clasped his hands together and said, "Well, ladies, I think we can work something out. Your first opportunity will probably be with McKenzie; he's a trader that comes through here regularly and is due back through just any day now. He travels with his wife and she'd be good company for you. If that's not suitable, I have some wagons goin' to Westport with some trade goods and to pick up some more. Usually, I make that trip in the spring but we've taken in some peltries that need to go back and we've had an unusual run on other goods that need resupplied. But, either way, we'll get you back east, at least to Missouri. I can't make any guarantees beyond that."

The three looked at one another and the sisters showed their happiness and expressed their thanks to Bent repeatedly. Owl Woman had prepared a meal of antelope steaks, potatoes and onions, and fried bread. Bent had arranged for the sisters to have a separate room and after they left the Bent's, they placed their few belongings in the room, eagerly anticipating a night in a bed. Tatum made his bed in another room, having agreed to meet the girls early at the trader's, and was soon out for the night.

The sisters' only attire was the buckskin tunics given by White Feather, but their clothing was not as important as it would have been a few months prior. But Tatum had a surprise for them and ushered them into the trader's to see what he had waiting for them. Arranged on the counter were several dresses and other ladies' attire. The trader explained, "Sometimes we get folks through that ain't got much to trade an' I'll take some o' their homespun stuff just to hep 'em out. Now, I ain't sure if any of it'll fit, but you just hep yoresef' an' then we'll settle up."

The girls were almost giddy as they rummaged through the piles of women's things and picked out several items that they thought would be suitable. They laid them aside and looked at Tatum as he stepped up and let the trader tally up the goods. As he was doing his sums, Tatum saw some pistols lying on the shelf behind the trader and leaned over for a better look. He was surprised to see two Paterson Colts lying together. He touched the trader on the arm and said, "Let me look at those Colt's yonder." The trader turned, picked up the two Paterson's and laid them on the counter in front of Tatum and looked up at the young man. Tatum said, "Add these to the bill, and some powder, caps, and lead and molds as well." The trader nodded, finished his tally and pushed the paper to Tatum. The young man took a leather pouch from his belt, counted out the proper coins and settled the bill.

When they exited the store, the sisters with their arms full, Tatum stopped and handed the pistols and gear and the pouch of coins to Val and said, "This is what was left among your family and the others at the wagons. It'll be enough to get you where you need to go, and more besides. Maybe even help you get a start back there; I'm sure they would all want that." The sisters looked at Tatum, surprised with his words and the pouch of coins, and Cat said, "It seems we're always saying thank you," she dropped her head, "and it's never enough."

"I'll be leaving a little later. I'm sure you're gonna be okay now, and Mr. Bent has promised to make certain of that. I'll come say good-bye before I leave," he said as he dropped his eyes from theirs. Cat said, "You better!"

He looked up and grinned and turned back to the trader to see to his own resupply. He wasn't sure about being able to say good-bye, but the mountains were calling and he was anxious to resume his journey.

As Tatum rattled off his list of needs, the trader stacked the goods on the counter. Tatum knew this would be his last supply until spring and he also knew he would have to be frugal in his use of these supplies; what with his funds dwindling and space on his packs limited, he was thinking about the coming winter and what he could do without. As he and the trader dickered over quantities and prices, Tatum heard a ruckus from in front of the store and looked up at the trader, expecting him to know what was happening. When the trader shrugged his shoulders, Tatum turned from the counter and started for the door. His horses were tethered in front of the store and he wanted to be certain there was no one pilfering from his packs.

With the trader right behind him, Tatum stepped through the door and stopped on the walkway when he saw a group of Cheyenne gathered to the side of his packhorse and chattering to one another, pointing to Tatum's packs on the big bay. He looked at his packs and quickly realized what they were excited about. The War Shield from Doh‰san of the Kiowa was beside the parfleche atop the packs. Tatum didn't carry it there for any other reason than the size of the shield gave no other option. But apparently the sight of the Kiowa war shield from a leader of the Kiowa, here in the midst of a band of Cheyenne, was alarming to those warriors that had fought against the fearsome Kiowa from south of the Arkansas River. The design of the shield, scalp locks, and pattern of decoration told the Cheyenne this was the shield of a chief of the Kiowa. When the Cheyenne warriors spotted the shield, they immediately thought that chief was among them.

Tatum casually strolled to the packhorse and began adjusting the packs, opening the panniers to ready them for his new purchases, and moving the shield aside to give access to the parfleche. His movements were just to show the Cheyenne that this was his horse and packs and the shield was his, not an enemy of their people. As he adjusted the packs, one of the Cheyenne saw the tomahawk at his belt and pointed it out to his fellow warriors. The band of observing warriors had fallen silent as they watched this young white man that carried a Kiowa war shield and wore a tomahawk of the Osage. Tatum chuckled to himself as he realized the impact these items made with the Cheyenne, for these things were more often taken in battle than given as gifts of friend-ship. Either way, they demanded respect. He thought, *I wonder what they'd do if I brought out the beaded belt from Buffalo Hump of the Comanche,* and chuckled to himself again.

He stepped back up on the boardwalk and followed the trader into the store to settle his bill and retrieve his goods. When he walked outside with his newly purchased goods, the crowd of Cheyenne had dispersed, and he packed his gear and goods without hindrance. He was just finishing tying things down when there was a bit of a ruckus at the gate and Tatum looked up to see an impressive figure on a big black horse with four white stockings and a blaze face lead two mule-drawn freighters into the plaza. A cloud of dust swirled around the wheels of the freighters and the hooves of the mules as he hollered with a voice that echoed from the adobe walls to announce his arrival, "Ho, Bent! Taylor McKenzie's back! And it's time for some Mezcal!"

McKenzie had a rotund figure that filled the saddle and a bushy red beard that covered the top half of his big chest. His broad shoulders stretched the fringed buckskin coat and his big arms and hands held the reins of his prancing horse before his chest. "Ho, Bent! Where are ye?" he hollered again, searching the doorways of the many rooms around the plaza waiting for his friend to appear.

"What's all the ruckus outchere?" came a familiar voice from under the overhang. William Bent leaned against one of the support posts and appeared to be trimming his finger-nails with a big Bowie knife, disinterested in the arrival of his long-time friend. He looked at McKenzie and let a broad grin cross his face as he said, "Did you say you were buyin'?"

"Aye, to be sure! And it's thirsty I am!" declared the big Scotsman as he swung down from his horse. He motioned to the buxom woman that watched from the seat of the first freighter and she began to climb down from her lofty perch. She was a dark skinned Mexican woman with long hair, held back from her face by a band of ribbon tied at the side. Attired in the traditional flowing skirt and peasant blouse of her people, her smile radiated with friendliness. She dropped to the ground and turned, holding her arms wide-spread as she walked toward Bent and said, "Billy, Billy, Billy, givea momma a beeg hug!" Bent stepped away from his leaning post and held open arms for Maria McKenzie and the two long-time friends embraced like brother and sister.

She stepped back, hands on hips and asked, "And where ees your woman? Where ees Owl Woman?"

Bent looked at Maria and said, "At the stove, where she belongs."

Maria cocked her head and squinted her eyes as she looked at him, and started to step around him, waving one hand in the air as she muttered, "Aiiiieee, you men! I should give all of you a good spanking!" She walked past him and into his quarters in search of her friend.

Tatum watched the two friends, McKenzie and Bent, walk up the steps to the room with the billiard table and the bar. He turned back to his task of tying down the gear on his packhorse. He was thinking about the sisters and knew their hopes were high about going with McKenzie's freighters back to Saint Louis, but nothing had been arranged. He looked to the upstairs room and decided to see if he could finalize the arrangements for the sisters.

As he entered the room, he was surprised how well lit the room was. With windows, though small, on all four walls, it was not the usual darkened room he was accustomed to seeing. He no sooner entered when he was hailed by William Bent and asked to join them. He reached for a chair and Bent introduced him to McKenzie with, "Tate, this is Taylor McKenzie, the biggest, loudest, and crookedest trader this side of the Mississippi!"

The big Scotsman laughed at the description and held out his meaty hand to shake and Bent continued, "Mac, this is Tate Saint, new to the mountains but he ain't no pilgrim."

Tatum extended his hand to have it swallowed by Mac's and the big Scotsman's smile parted the whiskers like a Clipper ship cutting the water. "Wal, an' it's always a pleasure to shake hands with a mountain man, even if ye are new to the woods."

"And it's good to meet you too, sir. I've heard about you from Mr. Bent here and I wanted to talk to you about your trip to St. Louis."

"Surely, you're not lookin' to leave these beautiful mountains already, are ye?"

Tatum chuckled at the response he had already heard from others, but answered, "Oh, it's not for me. There's a couple of ladies that need to go back east," and he was interrupted by Bent who started telling the story of the sister's survival with the Comanche. As he spoke, the Scotsman looked at Tatum and back at Bent, listening and nodding his head in disbelief. When Bent concluded, Mac looked at Tatum and said, "And ye did all that, didja?"

Tatum dropped his head, then looked back at Mac and said, "Well, my pa used to always say that the good Lord watches out for fools and young'uns so I guess I qualify on both counts."

Both Bent and Mac laughed at his response and Mac said, "Well, my young friend, you can set your mind at ease. My Maria, God bless her soul, will be tickled plum pink to have a couple o' young women to help her on the way back. An' unless I miss my guess, she'll mother 'em all the way."

Tatum grinned at Mac's response and as he stood to leave, he extended his hand to shake with both Bent and Mac and said, "Gentlemen, I thank you very much. It sure puts my mind at ease now. Thanks again."

As he walked away, he heard Bent start to tell his friend more about the young man he just met, but Tatum was unconcerned about their discussion. With the worry about the sisters relieved, he walked down the stairs and over to the door of the girls' room and knocked. The door opened wide to reveal the sisters standing side by side in their new dresses and showing broad smiles. "Tate! Come in, come in," said Val as she stepped back away from the door.

Tate walked in, smiling at the girls and took the only chair in the room as the sisters sat on the edge of the bed. Cat said, "So, how do you like our new dresses? A very handsome young man picked them out for us!" she declared coyly.

Tate laughed at her remark and answered, "You both look very nice. You're already looking like you belong in the city."

"I don't know about 'belonging' but at least we won't stick out like a sore thumb."

"Well, I've got good news for you. The trader that Mr. Bent spoke about pulled in a little bit ago, and I've talked to him and he said he would be glad to have you ladies go to St. Louis with him and his wife Maria."

The sisters looked at Tatum with sober expressions and didn't respond to the news like he expected. He thought sure they would be jumping for joy, knowing things were set for their return. But they sat silently until Val asked, "When do we leave?"

"In the morning. He's got a few things to unload and others to load, but they'll be ready to pull out at first light."

"And when are you leaving?" asked Cat.

"I'm pretty close to ready now. I prefer to travel at night but I figger to put some miles behind me 'fore night falls."

"So, really, you're here to say good-bye," said Val as she looked at Tatum.

"Well, yeah, I guess so," he mumbled, looking at the floor.

The sisters stood and walked toward him as he rose from the chair. They looked long at each other and Cat held her arms out for Tatum and he stepped into them. They hugged long and hard as Cat lay her head against the chest of her angel in buckskins, sobbed a little and finally pushed back to give her sister room. Val also gave Tatum a long embrace, placed her cheek against his chest and whispered, "You know we love you." Tatum nodded his head but didn't answer as Val stepped back to look up at her friend. Tears filled every eye and Cat dabbed at hers as Tatum dropped his head and wiped his on his sleeve.

"You can write when you get back. Just put my name and send it here to the fort. I'll probably come back through here sometime and pick up any letter you might send. I do want to know that everything's alright with the two of you."

The sisters leaned against each other and nodded to Tatum, choking back the sobs. He dropped his eyes and turned to leave. He looked back one time, smiled and said, "Sure gonna miss you two." As he pulled the door shut, he heard the girls let the sobs come as he choked back his own. He crossed the corner of the plaza to where his horses were tethered, slipped the reins from the hitch rail and stepped aboard his sorrel. He reined the gelding around, tugged on the lead rope of his packhorse and pointed them toward the main gate. As he neared the gate, he turned in his saddle to look back and seeing the girls standing in front of their door, he doffed his hat and waved. He grinned when they lifted their arms and waved back, holding on to each other. He dropped into his saddle and gigged his horse through the gate and kept his eyes on the distant mountains as he made for the crossing of the Arkansas to resume his journey.

CHAPTER THIRTY-SEVEN
MOUNTAINS

THE BIG MOON HUNG IN THE BLACK NIGHT AS A LAMP UNTO the path of the lone wanderer. He lifted his eyes to the sky, noting the position of different constellations his father had schooled him about. His favorite was Orion and the star at the tip of the hunter's sword was the one he always searched for as it was the favorite of his mother's. He dropped his gaze to the moonlit prairie before him and let his eyes trace the silhouette of the distant mountains in the Sangre de Cristo range. His first journey through these flats had taken him to the Spanish Peaks, but now his sights were set on the sentinel mountains that scratched the sky and marked the pass into the San Luis valley. His exploration of those peaks and the mountain range had just begun when he encountered the wagon train and he was forced to intervene in their travels.

But now there was nothing to deter him from his quest for winter quarters in the mountains. The long-held dream, treasured by both Tatum and his father, was to make a home in the mountains and he was determined to make that dream a reality. That dream had been put in jeopardy when he helped the members of the wagon train but, now, he was again on the trail to the Rockies.

For three days, Tatum never took his eyes off the mountains. Each mile increased his enthusiasm and eagerness to begin his search for his winter quarters. It was coming on morning with the pink of the dawn pushing its way past the flat horizon to the east and behind Tatum. He had been following the trail near the creek in the bottom and now looked for a camp among the aspen on the shoulder of the towering mountain.

Tatum was startled awake by the bugling of a bull elk somewhere up the side of the tall granite-topped peak. It was the first time he heard the unique challenging call of the royalty of the woods and when it sounded again with the high-pitched squeal followed by several grunts, Tatum grinned at the recognition of the bull's bugle. Carson had said it was the prettiest sound of the mountains, and a sure sign that fall was coming.

Tatum rolled from his blankets and stood and stretched, sucking in the cool pine-scented air of the mountains and grinned as he looked around. Below him and to the east, the flats of the plains stretched as far as he could see, but behind him he could see the towering peaks of the Sangre de Cristo. Movement near the creek bottom caught his eye and he stepped from the trees to look below. A herd of elk was strung out along the creek bottom, pushed by a herd bull at the back, and Tatum guessed there were more than seventy head of elk. He had never witnessed such a mass of wild animals in his life and he stood and stared at the astounding sight. He thought, *What an amazing country this is,* and he shook his head in wonder as he watched the long-legged animals disappear into the black timber.

Tatum turned back to his camp, considering what he had seen and what the day before him held. Carson had warned him to begin his preparations for the winter as soon as possible and now with the cool breeze from the mountains tugging at his collar, he knew time was wasting and he needed to get busy.

He thought about his plans as he waited for the coffee to perk, thinking about whether to try and find a cave or over-hang or to just get busy and start a cabin. He knew it would be more than just finding shelter; he would have to provide for his horses and himself. He also knew he had a lot to learn about living in these mountains but for now that meant laying in a supply of grass and such for the horses and a goodly supply of meat for himself. He stood and looked around his camp, and began to wonder if this undertaking was more than he could handle. But he grinned at the thought and reminded himself this wasn't just planning for a camp. This was fulfilling a dream, the dream held dear by him and his father. And a dream required a lot of work, but it takes a dream to make life worth living.

He laughed out loud and started packing up. He was going to count this as the first day of the realization of his dream. He was in the Rocky Mountains and it couldn't get much better than this. Little did he know what was in store for him as he mounted up and started his search.

A LOOK AT FRONTIER FREEDOM

ROCKY MOUNTAIN SAINT BOOK 2

Tatum Saint and his father shared a dream of the Rocky Mountains, but when his father was killed, young Tatum decided to make that dream a reality. But wherever he goes, there's always somebody needing help. Now as he prepares to build a cabin in the wilderness, he stumbles across a couple of runaway slaves that were seeking freedom in the uncharted territory. After their camp is destroyed and brother and sister are injured when Tatum stampedes a herd of elk, he feels obligated to care for them until they recover. Tatum finds it an arduous process to settle in the mountains, with confrontations with the Caputa Ute, mountain lions, and grizzly bears. But when the Jicarilla Apache take the girl and his friend, White Feather of the Comanche, captive, he and her brother, together with Tatum's friends from the Comanche, must mount a rescue. Using their own superstitions against them to balance the odds, the challenges and confrontations prove to be deadly and overwhelming. But not only must they battle the dreaded Apache, they must also face the assaults of nature herself, not just to rescue the captives, but to survive as well. It is a hard lesson to learn that freedom in the frontier does not come easily nor without great cost.

AVAILABLE APRIL 2018

GET YOUR FREE STARTER LIBRARY

Join the Wolfpack Publishing mailing list for information on new releases, updates, discount offers and your FREE Wolfpack Publishing Starter Library, complete with 5 great western novels:

http://wolfpackpublishing.com/receive-free-wolfpack-publishing-starter-library/

ABOUT THE AUTHOR

Born and raised in Colorado into a family of ranchers and cowboys, B.N. Rundell is the youngest of seven sons. Juggling bull riding, skiing, and high school, graduation was a launching pad for a hitch in the Army Paratroopers. After the army, he finished his college education in Springfield, MO, and together with his wife and growing family, entered the ministry as a Baptist preacher.

Together, B.N. and Dawn raised four girls that are now married and have made them proud grandparents. With many years as a successful pastor and educator, he retired from the ministry and followed in the footsteps of his entrepreneurial father and started a successful insurance agency, which is now in the hands of his trusted nephew. He has also been a successful audiobook narrator and has recorded many books for several award-winning authors. Now finally realizing his life-long dream, B.N. has turned his efforts to writing a variety of books, from children's picture books and young adult adventure books, to the historical fiction and western genres

https://wolfpackpublishing.com/b-n-rundell/